Praise for *The Case of Windy Lake*:

**USBBY (The United States Board on Books for Young People)
2020 Outstanding International Books List**

"These tweens are smart, curious, and resourceful."

—JEAN MENDOZA,
AMERICAN INDIANS IN
CHILDREN'S LITERATURE (AICL)

"The Muskrats feel like the kind of real kids that have been
missing in children's books for quite some time."

—QUILL & QUIRE

"Chickadee's rez-tech savvy pairs well with her cousin
Otter's bushcraft skills, and, along with Atim's brawn and
brother Samuel's leadership, the four make a fine team. …an
Indigenous version of the Hardy Boys full of rez humor."

—KIRKUS REVIEWS

"Their makeshift fort in a rusted-out school bus has the appeal
of the Boxcar Children's titular boxcar, and in fact there's
overall an old-fashioned classic mystery feel along with a look
at contemporary rez life in this first installment of a series."

—THE BULLETIN OF THE
CENTER FOR CHILDREN'S BOOKS

"[A] smart and thought-provoking mystery for middle grade
readers."

—FOREWORD REVIEWS

THE CASE OF THE MISSING AUNTIE —
BOOK TWO IN THE MIGHTY MUSKRATS SERIES:

THE MIGHTY MUSKRATS ARE ON A NEW CASE IN THE BIG CITY

The Mighty Muskrats are off to the city to have fun at the Exhibition Fair. But when Chickadee learns about Grandpa's missing little sister, who was scooped up by the government and adopted out to strangers without her parents' permission many years ago, the Mighty Muskrats have a new mystery to solve.

THE CASE OF WINDY LAKE

<<< **A MIGHTY MUSKRATS MYSTERY** >>>
BOOK ONE

THE CASE OF WINDY LAKE

MICHAEL HUTCHINSON

Second Story Press

Library and Archives Canada Cataloguing in Publication

Hutchinson, Michael, 1971-, author
The case of Windy Lake / Michael Hutchinson.

(Mighty Muskrats mystery)
ISBN 978-1-77260-085-8 (softcover).—
ISBN 978-1-77260-116-9 (hardcover)

I. Title.

PS8615.U827C37 2019   jC813'.6   C2018-905146-9

Edited by Gillian O'Reilly and Kathryn Cole

Sixth printing 2021

Printed and bound in Canada

*Second Story Press gratefully acknowledges the support
of the Ontario Arts Council and the Canada Council for the Arts for
our publishing program. We acknowledge the financial support of the
Government of Canada through the Canada Book Fund.*

 **ONTARIO ARTS COUNCIL
CONSEIL DES ARTS DE L'ONTARIO**   Canada Council   Conseil des Arts
for the Arts   du Canada

Funded by the Government of Canada
Financé par le gouvernement du Canada |  Canada

MIX
Paper from
responsible sources
FSC® C103567

Published by
Second Story Press
20 Maud Street, Suite 401
Toronto, Ontario, Canada
M5V 2M5
www.secondstorypress.ca

To my grandparents, Dan and Angelique Cook,
my many cousins, and my daughters,
Emerald and Lily.

CHAPTER 1

A Missing Bone-digger

"They're not even sure where he went missing from! Where do you start tracking?"

Uncle Levi sat across from Grandpa at the table. With a deep sigh, he pulled at a fold in the lapel of his Windy Lake Police Service uniform and leaned forward. He studied the wrinkled face of the old man.

Samuel and Chickadee worked around the two men. Sam was scooping ashes out of the wood stove. Chickadee kept the men's tea warm and cups filled. The old man was silent for a considerable time. "Think like him," he said.

Uncle Levi looked at the lake outside the wide window in Grandpa's kitchen. He shook his head a little.

"Hard to say to a company boss from down south."

The children tiptoed around the kitchen as their Elders talked. They knew they were hearing the Mighty Muskrats' next mission, and causing too much noise would get them sent outside. Grandpa motioned to his cup. Chickadee filled it.

"What was his name?"

"Dr. Troy Pixton. He's an archeologist, hired by the mining company." The kids could see that the newest issue on the First Nation was stuck in their uncle's mind like a rock in a moccasin.

"What do they need with a bone-digger?" Grandpa frowned.

"It's part of the mining company's contract with the community. They have to do historical assessments of the places where they're going to build a new building or prospect in a new place. The archeologist checks out the area, does a few exploratory digs, and then digs deeper if they find anything. They usually don't."

"Or they never say."

"Well, that's what all the traditionalists say. And those crazy activists. Who knows what's true?"

The old man chuckled.

The thick, wood door of the ancient house creaked loudly. Atim and Otter stepped in from outside. Each boy had an armful of chopped logs and sticks for the wood box.

Their uncle nodded at the boys.

"That granddaughter of yours is their war chief," Uncle Levi said to his father. He took off his police cap, scratched his head, and then replaced the hat.

"Who's a war chief?"

"Denice." Uncle Levi sounded slightly annoyed.

"She's your niece." Grandpa looked at his son.

Uncle grunted in acceptance.

"You know why she fights like that," Grandpa gently chided his son. "Your brother lived fast and hard. He partied too much. Denice rebelled by devoting her life to taking care of him. I don't have to tell you that."

Uncle Levi nodded in grudging agreement.

"To take care of him…she had to go to the same rough places he did, stay up as long as he did, be out all night with the same people he was. She became rough and tough too, trying to take care of her dad. And when he passed, she had no one to take care of anymore. So, she turned outwards." Grandpa leaned toward his son, looking into his eyes. "You know she will do much for our community, if she can turn her strength to a good cause."

Uncle Levi nodded but stared out the window at the lake.

The sound of logs tumbling from the boys' arms into the wood box drew everyone's attention. Grandpa seemed to notice the children for the first time, but they all knew he had just been waiting until all their chores were done. With a wave of his hand he dismissed them. "All right. Go outside, rez puppies."

The kids left the small house in a rush. They were inseparable, and they had been given the name Mighty

Muskrats by their oldest uncle who had watched them laugh, fight, poke, and snap at each other as they grew up. The nickname had spread across the First Nation and each of their exploits added to the Mighty Muskrats' reputation.

"We have to find him!" Chickadee urged her cousins as they walked up the gravel road. Her smile beamed from a scattering of freckles sprinkled across pudgy cheeks. Long black hair fell over her wide shoulders.

"What are you talking about?" Atim was the largest of the group and the oldest. With his muscles and long legs, he could easily outrun his cousins and his brother, Samuel. Ever since his parents had moved their family to the reserve, Atim had been growing out his hair, but it had yet to touch his shoulders and it often hung in his eyes. He moved it away with a flick of his head.

The sometimes leader of the group, Samuel, rubbed his chin, trying to squeeze out as much info as he could from what he had heard in the house. "Some city archeologist must have got lost. Uncle Levi has to find him." With his thin frame and short cropped hair, Sam bounced down the road as though his big head was pulling him along.

"We should!" Atim declared. He tingled with excitement at the thought. With most of spring break still ahead of them, there was plenty of time to figure out where the missing bone-digger was. They walked a little faster.

Otter's parents had died in a car accident when he was young. He had been raised mostly by their grandpa and had spent a lot of time with the old man learning bushcraft and the teachings of their people. He was the smallest of the Mighty Muskrats but in many ways the toughest.

Otter stopped and studied the sky. It was a beautiful spring day, a big change from the storm the day before. After a moment's reflection, he jogged to catch up to his cousins.

"Let's go to the fort!" Chickadee began to run. "I can check him out on the Internet."

The boys followed.

The Windy Lake First Nation was on the shores of the great lake that gave the community its name. Although the First Nation made up the bulk of the community, the Métis and Canadian community just off the reserve was starting to grow. The houses and neighborhoods of Windy Lake were scattered amidst evergreens and outcroppings of ancient limestone.

Back in the 1950s, an open pit mine had opened up near the community. An energy generating station and dam had been built on a nearby river to provide electricity to the facilities. The pollution from the mine and the changing of the water levels by the dam had been the source of much conflict in the area.

When the cousins' parents were teens, officials at the government department that ran First Nation communities had noticed that First Nations in Canada were often in remote locations. These places would be perfect draws for tourists and thrill seekers they decided.

In Windy Lake, a hotel had been constructed, the local snake pits fancied up, and a new dock for visitors' boats was built. The community was told to drag the nonfunctioning vehicles scattered across the rez to a central location away from the highway and tourist spots. The tourists and their money never showed up. But the field of stacked, old vehicles became a gathering place for the discarded metal, electronics, and appliances that seemed inappropriate in the garbage dump.

The kids looked around for watching eyes before they headed to a Bombardier within the pile of cars, trucks, and other vehicles. The Bombardier was a cross between a van and a snowmobile. The big box for the driver and engine rested on skis and tracks, so it could get through the snow. This one had been abandoned for years.

The Mighty Muskrats opened the door to the old blue snow-van and climbed inside. The interior of the faded Bombardier was a kid's heaven. Posters lined the walls. Cushions and blankets lined the benches. But they clambered past them, opening a screen that originally separated the riding compartment from the engine. Instead of a motor, there was the gaping maw of an aluminum culvert. The metal tunnel led between two pillars of old cars and farther into the junkyard. Boards covered with old carpets lay along its bottom. The kids crouched and crawled into the tunnel. Otter closed the metal screen that hid the tunnel behind him.

The other end of the culvert was stuck into the emergency door of a school bus. The long vehicle was buried in the pile of cars. Couches replaced most of the bus seats, a dining table and chairs were pushed against one wall, and a laptop computer blinked on a table in front of a sofa. Long ago, the kids had snaked an electrical cord to their sanctuary from a nearby hydro pole.

Chickadee took a Wi-Fi adapter from her pocket and plugged it into her computer's USB port. In a moment, she was searching for the doctor's name.

"Troy Pixton...Troy Pixton...Troy Pixton...come to me, Troy Pixton."

The boys giggled.

"Shhh!" Chickadee scolded. But she broke into a grin as her attention shifted back to the screen.

The boys moved farther into the bus.

"Probably not the cricket player.... Wow! A lot of people know him," she cried. "Probably not the psychiatrist from the States."

Samuel slumped into the driver's seat and took his current read from off the thin dash. Knickknacks and interesting items from the refuse outside covered the bus's hood and filled the view through the missing windshield.

The trunk of an overturned car sat in front of the bus, which prevented anyone from seeing in or out.

Atim went to a discarded set of weights closely gathered around an incline bench that was screwed together from mismatched pieces. Otter quietly picked up a battered guitar leaning against the wall and pulled out one of the dining chairs. His fingers began to play over the strings.

"Here he is," Chickadee spoke. "Degree in anthropology and archeology from Victoria University.... Dr. Pixton has written *Oral History: Smoke or Mirror?* and *Canada Had a Spirit and Intent Too! Treaty-making in the Late 1800s.* He was the head of the Native Studies Department at the University of Alberta."

"Sounds like he's anti-Indian." Sam shook his head. "An archeologist who doesn't like the cultures he's studying."

"Doesn't seem that weird when you consider he's hired by the mining company." Atim curled a barbell.

"Maybe that's where we should start...at the company office." Chickadee swiveled her chair until she was facing the boys. They nodded in agreement.

"Sounds good." Samuel snapped his book shut.

Otter stopped playing guitar and they got ready to leave the fort. Once they were back in the Bombardier snow-van, they surveyed the land outside its rounded windows.

"Do you see anybody?" Atim asked as he flicked his hair out of his eyes. The other Muskrats shook their heads in turn.

With the area clear, they quickly tumbled out into the sunshine. Through the tall, dead grass from last summer that surrounded the junkyard, they followed a trail to the road.

The walk through the rez was unseasonably warm and humid. A thin layer of black soil, thickened by eons of decaying foliage, was easily scratched, revealing a hard bed of white limestone mud. The high points of the reserve were outcroppings of rock slowly being shaped by erosion. The children's community had been cut out of an evergreen forest that eked out a living on an inch of topsoil.

"I can't wear anything black! I just got this hoodie and it's already full of white mud!" Chickadee shouted at no one.

"It's a conspiracy to turn us white." Atim chuckled.

"We'd be drowning now if we were back in the time it was made. This was a big lake bed ten thousand years ago." Sam studied the road.

"Doesn't help me now! I need to be clean today!" Chickadee rolled her eyes.

The boys laughed.

They walked past crumbling homes; built according to government plans, erected by lowest bidders. The only variety in the houses was the decade they were built and their state of repair. That stretched from condemn-able to could-use-a-good-paint.

In time, they turned off the road and down a trail that entered a smattering of forest. The houses of the reserve were scattered along a stretch of highway and not in the neat rows of the Métis half of the community or the trailer park. It was not uncommon to come across a patch of wilderness between neighborhoods on the rez. In the shadows of the thin, but tall, pines the temperature dropped to a chill. The kids walked a little quicker.

A scream cut the air.

Otter stopped. "Hear that?"

A woman's angry outburst once again sliced through the quiet of the bush.

The Mighty Muskrats looked at each other and then took off running.

CHAPTER 2

A Community in Conflict

Through the trees, a horn blast from a large truck was met with shouts and curses. The kids bounded off their short-cut and back onto the road. Rounding the corner, they saw a large dump truck trying to exit the mining company compound. It was slowly nudging its way through a small crowd of people. Protestors pounded on the truck with homemade signs. Others pushed ineffectively against its relentless bumper. The owner of the scream was now leading the mini-mob in a chant.

"What do we want!" The megaphone barked the words of their older cousin, Denice. Her long, dark hair hung over a camouflage jacket.

"Consultation!" the protestors shouted back.

"What's it gotta be?" Denice tapped the shoulder of a man pushing against the front of the truck. He stood up and hoisted his sign.

"Meaningful!" they cried in unison as the big truck crossed an unseen line, and the activists let it pass.

Samuel studied the mining compound as the other kids went to speak to their cousin. It was surrounded on three sides by a high fence. On the side along the river, there were always great barges leaving and arriving from the mining site. Cranes along the pier loaded the ore from the barges into dump trucks. From long observation Sam knew, an hour after a boat docked, at least one truck would drive around the big warehouse that held the company office at one end and leave through the gate. Sam joined the other Muskrats but kept a close eye on the office door.

Denice was fired up, but she always had time for her little cousins. Chickadee hugged her tightly before asking if she knew that a city-guy was missing.

"I didn't know he was lost. Rumor has it that he's found something big, but who knows? We sure ain't going to let him take it out of here. That's all I can say. Do you remember what Grandpa told us about The Chief?"

The kids nodded.

About fifteen generations before, a great chief on his deathbed asked his people to throw a stick on his grave each time they walked by. By the 1950s, that pile of twigs had grown to the size of a house. At that time, with the mine on the way, the provincial university had sent an archeologist to survey the area for places and objects of historic significance. The bone-digger heard about The Chief, and in the darkness of night, stole his bones and all the tools and weapons he'd been left with. Although the theft happened when their grandparents were kids, the event remained a scar on the community's relationship with Canada and the university.

"This theft of our history and our resources and our ceremonies has to stop! Hey, little cousins?" Denice's sentences always seemed to start out angry but ended with a smile. The Muskrats loved her dearly as she was fiercely protective of her family, especially the younger ones. Denice was passionate about everything she did. She always made everyone feel cared for, but they knew it was dangerous to get her angry.

"We're looking for the archeologist." Chickadee watched her cousin's reaction.

"Your new case, hey?" Denice smiled. "Well, one day you guys will be protecting our land. This guy will make a great warrior." Denice pretended to punch Atim on the shoulder. He feigned a dodge and a counter blow.

"I'll follow in your footsteps, Dee." Atim smiled broadly.

Denice tousled his hair. "I know you will, big guy." Movement from the gate caught her attention. "But right now...I think you better get out of here."

Chickadee tried to figure out what her cousin was looking at. Beyond the fence, it looked like another truck was getting ready to leave. The driver stared at the protestors for a long time before he hopped into the truck's cab.

"What's up, Dee?"

"Hey, cuzzins, just go over there across the road. Just for a bit, okay?" She ran back to her protesting friends as the truck reached the gate. Ten large security guards lined up along the fence, five holding on to the wide gate.

The Mighty Muskrats watched the action as they slowly walked across the gravel road.

The company men held the gate tightly against the truck as it lumbered its way out. The protestors launched themselves against the metal behemoth as soon as it poked its hood through. A great groan seemed to go up from everyone involved in the struggle. A team of protestors chanted for proper consultation as the man-versus-machine shoving match continued.

A chorus of screams went up.

"She's going under!"

"She's under the tire!"

"Help her!"

The trucked lurched to a stop. The protestors crowded near one of the front wheels. The guards on that side forgot the fight and leaned in to see what was going on.

"NOW!"

Denice rose from the center of the tight wad of protestors. In unison, the activists attacked the gate.

Atim and Otter looked at each other and laughed as

the dozen or so skinny Native protestors wrestled with the five fat company guards. The gate swung back and forth between the combatants like a broken wing. The guards on the other side heeded the driver's warning too late, and the numbers won the tug of war for the chain-link fence. With a shout, a small mob of angry citizens poured across the company lot.

CHAPTER 3

Protest Hug of Steel

The security guards threw their hands in the air and watched the scramble of activists. But when the office door slammed open, they began to run toward the nearest trespasser. The mine manager, Mr. Makowski, roared, "Who the hell let those...morons into the compound! Don't just look at me, you idiots! Get them before they sabotage something!"

His messy hair looked like gray flames above the burning crimson of his face as he marched toward the gate.

The truck driver hopped out of the truck. "They tricked me!"

"What?"

"The protestors! They pretended someone got run over. When your men went to check it out, they broke and ran."

"Did you see who pretended to get hit?"

"No. I just heard them yell, 'She's hit!'"

The manager noticed the Muskrats and shouted, "Hey, you kids, get out of here!"

The cousins just smiled and stayed on their side of the road. Mr. Makowski pushed the rolled sleeves of his shirt farther up his forearm, debating whether to come over. But he forgot about the Muskrats when the fittest of the security guards returned with one of the protestors.

The twenty-something guard held up a chain. "He was trying to lock himself to the big gas tank with this."

"What the heck were you trying to do!" The veins stuck out on the manager's neck. He pulled the thin activist closer as he spat the words.

"Stop you from killing our land!" The protestor pushed against the big man's arms but couldn't free himself.

"Oh, you freakin' idiots! It's the twenty-first century!" Makowski's rant was interrupted by police sirens approaching down the road.

"Now we'll see if these Indian cops will arrest their own."

More guards brought their captors back to the gate. The manager studied each activist.

"How many were there?" His eyes bored into the senior guard.

"We don't know, sir. Nobody thought to count as they ran in."

"Is this all all of them?"

"Our guys are still checking."

"Damn!"

The big man paced back and forth as a police truck pulled up and crunched to a stop in front of the dump truck.

As Uncle Levi opened his car door, the manager marched up and shouted in his face.

"You're responsible for your own people! Why can't you control them?!"

The Mighty Muskrats watched as their Uncle stepped slowly out of his vehicle, fixed his belt, and swept his gaze around the site, the bush, and the horizon.

"Because they're people," he said.

He sighed when the company bigwig began to scream in his face again.

"We were told that the law would be followed! Well?! Where were you when these animals ripped down my gate?" Mr. Makowski was turning purple now.

Uncle Levi looked at the activists standing in a tight group guarded by company security. He shut the police-truck door and looked at the Muskrats. "Was your cousin here?"

The kids nodded as one and looked into the compound.

"All right." Their uncle gave them a smirk. "Get out of here. We don't need any more of the family in trouble."

Uncle Levi hitched up his belt and walked onto the company lot.

The manager followed close on his heels. "Their cousin? Who are those kids?! What do they have to do with this? Where the hell are you going?"

Uncle regarded the company man with a slightly sympathetic look. "You don't have them all. The most troublesome one is still in here."

Everyone watched the two as they headed toward the big building. The manager stewed as Uncle Levi sauntered. Scanning left and right, he searched the shadows and crannies of the yard.

The security guards turned their attention to the gaggle of activists. The two groups watched each other closely, but neither left the area around the gate and hulk of the delayed dump truck. The Muskrats watched. When the adults' backs were turned, they quietly slipped past the truck and through the wide gate.

Uncle Levi and the company man were heading past the low, wide warehouse that hid the docks, barges, and river. The kids quickly, but quietly, moved out of range of a guard's easy glance and followed the two authority figures. A shout of discovery was heard from behind the yellowish building as they neared the company offices at its end. Their uncle and Mr. Makowski quickly vanished around the corner. The Muskrats broke into a run. Behind them, a yelp announced that the guards had noticed their presence on the wrong side of the fence.

Behind the long warehouse was a wide pier with two docks that stretched out into the lake. The cranes worked steadily. The area was littered with steel boxes of various shapes and sizes. Posts dotted the edge of the pier for the barges and boats to tie to. One of the company men stood with his hands on his hips glaring down at something hidden behind a set of stacked crates.

Mr. Makowski cursed loudly when he saw what it was. When Uncle Levi caught up, he took off his hat, wiped his brow, then shook his head.

Unseen, the Muskrats slipped behind a pile of boxes. They jostled for position before they slowly peeked over the edge.

The first things they saw were the mine manager swearing, their uncle staring out over the water, and the company employee trying to hide his smile behind his hand.

Farther down, their activist cousin sat with her arms and legs wrapped around one of the thick mooring posts. Denice looked as quiet and serene as the calm water beside her. Her grasp around the post was reinforced by metal; her hands, past her wrists, were slipped into either end of a steel tube, securing her firmly in place. The Muskrats looked at each other and giggled. After her own laughter subsided, Chickadee shushed the others. "Let's listen!"

Once again, the kids watched from behind the crate. The security guards had stopped looking for them and gravitated to their manager.

Denice started screaming her activist slogans. "You can't drink money!"

"Cut her loose from there!" Mr. Makowski threw a hand in the air. A few of the gathering workers scurried to find tools that could meet the demand.

"First Nations are the defenders of the land...except for my Uncle Levi!"

Uncle Levi slowly shook his head. "You can't see her hands."

"There are greener alternatives!" Denice's voice was getting rough.

"What?" The manager was flustered.

Uncle was his usual calm self. "You can't cut through that pipe unless you know where her fingers are," he said.

"Mother Earth prefers green!"

"I don't care about her fingers!" the manager countered.

"I know," Uncle Levi rumbled. "That's why we're going to make a perimeter, and you and your men are going to stay out of it."

With his big police shoes, Uncle Levi paced off a ten-foot distance.

"Water is the blood of Mother Earth!" Denice kept up her message.

The manager lost his mind. "Are you freakin' kidding me? You're closing off half the pier! How are my men supposed to load the boats?"

"I want you and your men to stay outside that circle."

Uncle Levi was unruffled in the face of the manager's storm.

"Who is your supervisor?"

Uncle Levi smiled at the implied threat.

"Hell no, I won't go!" Denice's voice was growing hoarse.

Her uncle continued to ignore her.

"She's only tied to one post. There's plenty of room to get around her." He pointed at the circle made by the boxes. He noticed the Muskrats peering over the edge of one but said nothing.

"I'm going to have your job!" Makowski jabbed his finger in the air.

Uncle Levi hitched up his belt and chuckled. "She hasn't really blocked you at all has she?"

"Without water we die!" Denice screamed.

The Muskrats burst into giggles at their cousin's protest.

"Look…" Makowski bellowed.

"NO!" With all the cursing the manager had done, this was the first time the police officer had spoken sharply to him.

The men's eyes met.

"You look…" Uncle Levi's voice was serious and steady. He pointed again at the circle of boxes around Denice.

The manager took a deep breath and assessed the situation. "I suppose not."

Denice knew her uncle well enough to keep her mouth shut for the moment.

"We can leave these boxes here," Makowski conceded.

"Thank you. I realize that she's trouble." Uncle Levi's easy tone returned quickly. With a touch of annoyance, he added, "She's my niece."

"Really?" Makowski looked down at Denice.

"Really. But I'll go talk to her and if that don't work, I'll get my pop to come down and talk to her."

"We're just borrowing the Earth for our children!" Denice started again. The Muskrats exploded with laughter once again.

"Look...I don't care how this is resolved. But get it done. Time is money." The manager was still angry, but he suddenly thought it better to be respectful to their uncle. He stomped off, cursing at his crew as he directed them to be careful of Denice.

Uncle Levi hitched up his belt and set his eyes on his niece. He sighed again and shook his head. The Muskrats stepped out from their hiding place and approached.

Uncle Levi took a long look at the water before finally setting his eyes on Denice.

"So, what? What will get you to stop this?"

"I don't want them here," Denice said angrily. "They're supposed to follow the agreement, but they don't."

"They say they do."

"C'mon!" Denice urged her uncle. "Hardly anyone from here works at this stupid mine." She shook her head. "We fish…and they're going to kill the water."

"Okay." Their uncle sighed. "So, you're going to stay here…for how long?"

"I can go for days without food."

"Okay, days. It's something to tell the company."

"Who are you working for? Our people or the company?"

"I work for the people. And, right now, our community is officially for this project."

"They'll kill our water!"

Uncle Levi walked over to the kids. "Come with me."

After speaking with the manager and telling him that Denice might be there a couple of days, Uncle Levi ordered the Muskrats to hop into his truck.

He hitched up his belt before he got in.

CHAPTER 4

Fishing for Information

"She's on a vision quest." Grandpa chuckled as he thought about it. "She picked her wilderness."

"What do you mean, Grandpa?" Sam asked. They were once again at the old man's house. Chickadee and Sam leaned against the kitchen counter and listened to their Elders. Otter and Atim, preferring the outdoors, hung around in the yard.

The old man looked at his grandson. "Well, do you know what a vision quest is?"

"It's a test," Sam said eagerly. "A test to see if a child is ready to be an adult."

"Vision quests are the seeking of a vision. They're done for many reasons, but the first vision quest can be an important rite of passage." Grandpa paused as he felt a memory from his distant past. "Before young people go on their first vision quest, they are told about the great ones among their people, the heroes in their families, and other important teachings."

"And they don't get any food or water." Chickadee smiled. "That must be tough."

"Well…it is a test in many ways. After being told the stories, after some time in the sweat lodge, the youngster is put somewhere safe and alone. And there they stay for, sometimes, four days and they are given very little, if anything, to drink."

"Why, Grandpa?"

"For two reasons, I guess. At first, it's about testing your ability to say 'No' to yourself. Finding your vision is something that only the best piece of you can do, so you must first learn to say 'No' to the animal in you. The animal that thirsts, the animal that hungers, the animal that complains when it has to do homework." Grandpa smiled.

"What's the other reason?" Sam pinched his lip as he listened.

"To prepare you for your vision, which comes from above. Your body is of the Earth."

"And what do you see?" Sam asked eagerly.

"It depends on the vision you are seeking." Grandpa was pleased with his grandson's interest. "Hopefully, on their first vision quest, a young person will see how to contribute to their people. To see how their Creation-given talents are best able to serve their family and community."

"And how is Denice on a vision quest, Grandpa? Isn't it usually for boys?" Chickadee filled Grandpa's teacup as she spoke.

"Anyone can search for a vision, but it is true that it is usually a rite of passage for young men. Your cousin has had a rough life, but she has the heart of a leader. It is her struggle that gave her that strength."

"But she's not in the forest." Chickadee was matter-of-fact.

"No, but she is on her own. She is facing this... wilderness alone. She has chosen. Maybe this location is important to her vision." He shrugged his shoulders and then smiled. "Your cousin wants to test the company, but...that may not be all she gets." The old man chortled.

"Pops!" their uncle rumbled. "This isn't funny or... spiritual. She's just causing trouble."

The old man waved his empty teacup in the air.

"She's being a voice," he insisted.

"There're lots of others who think like her," Chickadee said as she refilled her Elders' teacups.

"No...I know." Levi shook his head.

The two men sat quietly, looking out over the yard and the lake beyond.

Finally, their uncle spoke.

"Will you talk to her?"

"A person on a vision quest needs to be told of the heroes in our family." Grandpa sounded certain.

Uncle Levi paused to say something, but instead he just sighed, and then rose to leave. "Just convince her to let them cut the tube that's covering her hands."

"I'll speak to her."

Uncle Levi motioned to the kids as he made his way out of the aged house.

Chickadee and Sam followed. The door complained loudly as it closed.

"This isn't helping find that missing archeologist, hey Uncle?" Chickadee was hoping he'd have some more information about their case.

Atim and Otter came around the corner.

"No, it isn't." Uncle Levi jumped as the receiver in his truck barked to life. He walked quickly to the vehicle, opened the door, and told the person on the other end to repeat themselves.

The radio cackled, "We need you back at the base, boss. They may have found that old man."

The Muskrats perked up and listened carefully. Their uncle noticed their interest and smiled. "Well, it looks like your new case may be solved, Muskrats."

The kids looked at each other, deflated.

"That's okay, Uncle." Sam shrugged.

"We're just happy he's been found." Chickadee looked at the ground, disappointed.

"Mm-hmm." Uncle smiled, hitched up his belt, and

rolled into the truck. With a wave, he pulled out of the driveway and drove off.

"What are we going to do now?" Atim tossed the hair from his eyes.

Chickadee shrugged.

"Let's go to the Station and see what people are saying," Sam suggested.

"That sounds like a good idea. I'm hungry," Atim enthusiastically agreed.

"You're always hungry," Chickadee teased. "Do we have any money?"

Otter pulled a handful of change out of his pocket.

Atim began to count it. "It's enough for some fries… maybe a pop," he said triumphantly.

"Super!"

"Let's go!"

The Station was more than just a gas station and a garage. It was also one of the four restaurants in town, it had a 24/7 convenience store, and it was one of the focal points of the moccasin telegraph. When the people were in a teasing mood, they often called it the Drama Station, but mostly, it was just the Station.

Chickadee breathed in the dusty, oily smell of the garage as they stepped into the gas station and store. Enticed by the prospect of french fries, Atim and Otter headed for the door leading to the restaurant.

Sam scanned the room. He nodded at the teenager

who was serving a highway-weary trucker. A few locals shopped the shelves, but there was nobody he was related to. He followed Chickadee and the others into the restaurant.

The jukebox was playing "Love Hurts" by Nazareth. Scarred and scuffed blue-and-once-white tiles covered the floor. Sun streamed in from large windows that overlooked the gas pumps, the parking lot, and the trucks buzzing north up the highway. Booths lined the other two walls. Tables and chairs were arranged in a semi-organized way across the checkered floor. Half the restaurant was occupied by First Nation people hunkered over cups of coffee. A few tables held non-local miners and highway travelers. Laughter was coming from most tables and jokes were being shared between a few. The quiet tables held smiling Elders.

One of the few local miners pointed at the kids, smiled, and then said something, which brought a laugh from his fellow employees. "Here come the Mighty Muskrats," the miner teased when they walked closer.

"Must be tough, working in a mine," Chickadee threw back.

"*Pfft*, we're on our week off. Two weeks in, one week out. It's THE life!" The men laughed.

"What do you guys know about that old man who got lost?" Sam liked a joke, but he was there for a reason.

So was Atim. "I'm going to order our fries," he

whispered in Chickadee's ear before he and Otter walked off to find a table.

"The Doc? He was an idiot. Educated guy, but stupid. I was on a crew that was waiting for him to finish but I didn't know him good. He didn't know the bush. I'm pretty sure he considered us savages!" He looked at his buddies as he said the last bit, and they chuckled at the dark joke.

"Who did work with him?" Sam interrupted.

"This one is always thinking," the local said to his crew, slightly annoyed. "Go talk to Ugly Fish. He was the Doc's gofer. I don't even think he was working for the mine. Just doing gofer stuff for that old man. He's over there. Look." Barry pointed with his lips.

Chickadee and Sam looked over to where the miner had gestured. Ugly Fish was sitting at a table with his sketchy cousins. Ugly Fish's real name was Moriah, which he insisted was from the Bible, but around here a "moriah" was an ugly fish. Most people called him "Fish", but they added the "Ugly" when they were being mean.

"Let's wait until he's by himself," Chickadee said to Sam.

They said their good-byes to the miners' table and joined Atim and Otter. The fries hadn't arrived yet. The boys were sharing a can of Coke.

"'Kay, we figure Fish may know something," Sam said as he slid into the booth beside Atim.

"We're going to wait until he's away from that crew before we ask him anything." Chickadee plopped down beside Otter. The Muskrats watched Fish's table. The waitress brought the fries with a second plate for Otter. He didn't like ketchup on top. He only liked to dip. The kids began to grab the potato sticks hungrily. The Coke was shared.

Eventually, Fish started saying good-bye to those he was with.

"Okay, he's leaving by himself," Chickadee whispered.

"That's good, hey?" Atim nudged her. She pushed him back.

"He may talk more if he's alone," Sam answered Atim.

Fish eventually limped across the restaurant and out the door. The Muskrats gulped down the last of the chips and followed.

"Hey, Fish!" Atim called.

The young man turned to see who called his name. Although Fish was only in his thirties, he seemed haggard. An old boating injury caused him to limp and slouch forward slightly. His hand-me-down clothes didn't fit well.

"What do you kids want?" He began to walk away as he asked the question.

"Did you hear they found that old man?" Sam asked, trailing after him.

"The Doc?"

"That's what we hear," Chickadee chimed in.

"We heard you were helping him out...with his science." Sam thought flattery might loosen Fish's lips.

"Yeah...yeah, I was. Took him out to his sites and even to a few others. He was excited about something."

"Which places?" Chickadee tried to sound only vaguely interested.

"You know...the tourist sights: the rock paintings along the river, the old winter site, the old fishing weir... couple of others. He thought they were fantastic." Fish laughed. "But I heard they *didn't* find him."

"Didn't find him?" Surprised, Sam looked at Chickadee.

"Who told you that?" she probed.

"Stu brought the RCMP boat down here on the trailer to fill up its tanks. He said they found the old guy's boat down by the delta. Said it looked like he just walked into the bush."

Fish stopped and turned to see why the kids were suddenly quiet. All he could see was four little clouds of dust as the Mighty Muskrats disappeared across the parking lot and down the bush trail.

CHAPTER 5

Chuckles at the Cultural Camp

The boat pounded against the waves as it cut through the lake. Otter sat at the front. Spray washed his face as the prow bumped across the water. Behind him, his cousins searched wave and shore for signs of another boat. Steering the fishing boat was their older cousin, Mark, who worked with their Uncle Bruce pulling nets.

The delta that Fish had spoken of was at the mouth of Snake Creek, a thin trickle that occasionally slithered out to form a broad stream when the spring rains came. When it was flooded, the fast-moving water picked up a lot of silt. When it dumped that soil at the creek's end, it created a small fan of swamp and mud that slowly pushed into the lake.

The delta was about a ninety-minute boat ride from town. Mark said he could take the kids as long as they stopped at the culture camp to drop off some ducks he had shot.

"Hey!" Atim yelled and pointed.

The traditionalists' camp had just come into a view. Not much could be seen, just flashes of color amidst the black and gray trunks of thin evergreens. There were several motorboats pulled up along the shore.

The landing site was filled with countless multi-colored stones slowly being ground into sand by the motion of the waves. Mark killed the engine and lifted the prop out of the water. Only the slap of waves could be heard until the pebbles began their subtle scratching as the ground came up to meet the aluminum bow.

Otter leapt into the knee-deep, clear water with the boat's rope in hand. With the help of the occasional lift from the waves he pulled his cousins farther into shore and tied the rope to a tree.

"Holee!" Mark exclaimed. "They've been raising the water at the dam. Look at what it did to the shore there." The frequent raising and lowering of the lake's water by the nearby hydro dam had eroded the bank of soil above the now wider strip of pebbled shore.

"I've never had to tie up this high before." Otter looked worried.

With everyone disembarked, they began the trudge up the hill to the camp.

Mark and Otter carried the ducks.

The traditionalists' camp was a group of teepees, wigwams, and shacks scattered amongst the trees in the sparse, spruce forest. Most of the teepees were painted with the colors and patterns of the people that owned them.

A few small cooking fires burned here and there, but the Muskrats headed for the fire in the center of the camp where the old men hung out, and where most of the visiting took place. Two old couples relaxed in lounge chairs, sipping their tea in the warmth of the flames.

Mark, being the oldest cousin, had the responsibility of speaking first. He presented his ducks to the Elders. Chickadee touched the arm of one of the older ladies and pulled up a stump of wood near her. Sam smiled at everyone and also sat on a section of tree trunk. Atim and Otter went to the nearby pile of firewood. Otter began to cut kindling with an ax as he listened to the conversation.

"Give two of those ducks to Grace. Her old man is in town, but he's coming back with their kids." A lady Elder lip-pointed toward Grace's camp.

"I'll take one." Her husband laughed. "I've been craving duck soup."

"You don't make good duck soup," his wife teased.

"I didn't say I was craving *my* duck soup."

"So, whose duck soup are you craving?" The old lady pretended to be angry. "Are you craving another woman's soup?"

The Elders, Muskrats, and Mark giggled. A quiet moment passed after the chuckling subsided.

"I hear they found that missing archeologist by the delta," Sam offered.

"What?" The old men were suddenly attentive. Sam was a little surprised by the level of focus.

"Yeah…. Fish told us. Said the cops found his boat by the delta…or somebody did."

"Did you tell your grandfather this?" One of the old men poked the fire as he spoke.

"We didn't have time…." Chickadee also felt the tension in her Elders. "We wanted to check it out."

One of the old women leaned forward. "Well…we want you to check it out too. Then come back and tell us what you saw. Tell us everything."

"Why do you want to know?" Sam felt it was more than idle curiosity.

"I saw that little old white man, wearing his blazer in the bush." The wrinkled Elder shook his head. "It sounds funny to think of him as dangerous. But to us, those bone-diggers can be worse than the miners. They want to turn our sacred places into money-making ventures like nobody else. If the miners want our sacred land, it is usually just by coincidence, but the bone-digger makes money from…us…our stories, our ancestors' places."

"I know about the old camp…and the old dancing site. Do you mean places like those?" Chickadee felt they were on the edge of a secret.

"Yes, places like those...." The old people shared a glance.

"There is nothing that I know of by the delta." Chickadee pushed.

The old woman beside Chickadee gave her a nudge. With a gentle smile she said, "Maybe you haven't earned that knowledge yet."

That put an end to the questions.

"Be careful as you go, young ones." One of the Elders stood. "It's getting late in the day. If you cannot get back to us, don't worry. Tell your grandfather. We'll hear about it eventually."

With quick good-byes and promises to return, the Muskrats and Mark were soon leaving the community fire and making their way back to the boat. Otter pushed them off the shore and they were soon pounding across the waves.

CHAPTER 6

A Rope Points the Way

As they approached the delta, the Muskrats could see an RCMP patrol boat with its front end pushed lightly into the mucky silt and the First Nation's police boat bobbing just offshore. An old yawl was stuck in the mud a short distance away from the open water. It was the fishing boat that was sometimes rented out by the Métis fisherman, Mr. Mackie.

Sam said to no one, "That must have been the archeologist's ride."

Mark cut the motor, and Otter and Atim pulled out paddles to slow the boat's coasting.

"Don't worry, boys, these waves and current will push us up into the soft mud. The hard part will be getting out." Mark kept an eye on Windy Lake's floating police cruiser. "Howdy!" he yelled at the officer in the boat. The band constable, Gus, was an old friend of Uncle Levi and their family.

"Hey. What are you kids doing here?"

"We heard they found that company man." Sam shaded his eyes from the sunlight as he spoke.

"Found his boat, or the boat Mackie rented him, but we have no idea where he is." A wood match danced from side to side in Gus's mouth.

"No tracks?" Atim leaned his head to get the hair out of his eyes and pointed at the rocky shore about a football field away from where they were parked on the edge of the delta's silt.

"There must have been some...but in this muck they disappear. It's practically quicksand. But he did get out... the shore rope was pulled out across the muck."

The black-and-yellow, nylon rope that would usually secure the rental boat to shore was, instead, stretched out to its full length across the mud. It looked as though someone had tried to pull the yawl toward the distant rocks.

"How do you know he didn't sink?" Sam looked over the bow.

"At this point...we don't." Gus studied the mud between the boat and the farther shore. "Your uncle is on the way with a dog...and Jerry is out there now with the probe."

Jerry was the RCMP officer from the patrol boat on the delta. He was wearing hip waders that went up to his armpits, which was a good thing because he sank up to his waist in the silty mud. He probed the area around the rental boat with a long rod. An older officer directed him from within the patrol boat.

Sam leaned toward Chickadee. "There isn't any mining stuff anywhere near here."

"I was thinking of that. I know the snake pits are back there. But Grandpa's never shown me anything other than that."

Sam shook his head to indicate he'd never been introduced to anything sacred or culturally significant in this area either. "Otter! He ever take you anywhere special back in the bush?"

Otter shook his head. He was the most bush savvy of the Muskrats. His grandfather used him as a fire keeper during the sweat lodge and other ceremonies when the older cousins weren't around.

They sat in silence and watched the RCMP officer struggle in the muck.

"Look at that. That's why there's no tracks. It just sucks them up." Gus shook his head.

"Did you check the hard shore?" Atim looked in the direction of the distant rocks.

"Well, we hope the dog will pick something up over there, but if not, we'll need volunteers to walk the bush." Gus's tone suggested he didn't want it to go that far.

In the distance, the approaching drone of a boat motor could be heard. The group turned to see who was coming.

Uncle Levi had just cleared the last point of land between them and the rest of the lake.

"Good. The dog." Gus went to the other end of his boat to tell the federal cops.

"Are we going to get in trouble for being here?" Mark looked at the Muskrats. He had been unwittingly pulled into their adventures before, and it hadn't always gone well for him.

As one, the Muskrats shrugged.

They watched the approaching boat.

Eventually, Uncle Levi slowed his engine to coast toward them. He seemed more annoyed than angry when he noticed the young ones. The Muskrats sighed with relief. They could work with annoyed. Sam looked at Chickadee and gave her a nod.

Chickadee went to the back of the boat. In a sing-song voice she said, "Hi, Uncle! Did you bring Scout?"

Frantically, the German shepherd bounced back and forth around the slowly moving patrol boat.

"How did you know?" Uncle Levi chuckled. He tried, unsuccessfully, to calm the dog.

They all laughed. Uncle Levi steered his slow-moving boat past them so he could speak to the RCMP.

"How's it going fellas?"

"It's tough slogging." The older policeman seemed to welcome the conversation. The younger officer looked up at his superior standing in the boat with consternation, shook his head, and then continued to struggle in the silt.

"Well, we're going with the dog back over there," Uncle Levi pointed along the rocky shore, "where we can pull the boats up on solid land. Then we'll follow the shoreline. See if we can pick up a scent."

After some further small talk with the RCMP and Gus, Uncle Levi restarted his engine and slowly pulled away from the shore.

"You three," he lip-pointed to Mark, Sam, and Chickadee, "go tell the Elders and Grandfather that we may need volunteers. Tell them to wait until I call, but to have their people ready."

He pulled his boat alongside theirs.

"You two come with me." He motioned to Atim and Otter. The two boys hopped into their uncle's boat and smiled back at their cousins.

The Muskrats were excited to be given jobs by their uncle.

"'Kay, go!" Uncle Levi chuckled. He pushed the throttle, and the powerful police boat surged into the waves.

Mark waved at Gus. "You heard the man. We're out of here."

As Mark started the engine and slowly steered away, Chickadee and Sam watched the older RCMP officer struggle to stay clean as he attempted to help the younger officer into their boat.

CHAPTER 7

The House-taurant

Back on the rez, after talking to the Elders at the cultural camp, Chickadee and Sam found Grandpa's house locked up and his truck gone.

"Where do you think he is?" Sam asked.

Chickadee shrugged. "Let's head to the Station but stop at the House-taurant on the way."

If the Station was an intersection of gossip in the area, the House-taurant was the heart of second-hand information on the rez.

The eatery's owner and chef, Mavis, had moved into her basement and turned her house into a coffee shop. Her dining room and living room were filled with mismatched tables and chairs. A large freezer hummed in the corner. Music was supplied by a portable CD player, its speakers mounted in the upper corners of a wall. A floor-model TV painted fuzzy pictures of the urban world across its screen.

A bell tinkled as the kids opened the door. The House-taurant was empty. The sound of the bell brought Mavis up from downstairs.

"What are you two up to?" she asked the kids. She motioned with a cigarette to her usual spot near the kitchen. The table held an ashtray, a cribbage board, and a weathered deck of cards. The usual condiments were lined up on the end by the wall.

"We're looking for Gramps." Sam sat down as he spoke.

"Do you want coffee?"

"Mmmm…just some water," Chickadee said. Sam nodded.

Mavis poured two glasses of water at her kitchen sink and brought them back. She lowered her sizable bulk into her chair and flicked her smoke at the ashtray.

"Pretty quiet, so far today. What have you Muskrats been doing?" Mavis studied the kids. She was a good listener, so people talked to her. She knew everything on the rez.

"They found that old man's boat," Sam announced with a grin.

"Did they find him?"

"Not yet." Chickadee gulped air as she finished a slug of water.

"Hmmm…." Mavis shifted in her chair. "Where's the boat?"

"Out by the delta," Chickadee offered.

The kids knew they had to give her something big if they wanted to find out anything in return.

"They may be looking for volunteers soon." Sam knew this was official information Mavis could spread. It was a sizable pelt of gossip.

"That's sorta interesting." Mavis feigned a lack of interest. "People will want to help out."

"Well…they should wait until Uncle Levi gives them the go-ahead. He's out by the snake pits with a dog right now. Hopefully, he'll find the bone-digger."

"If they do need volunteers, they may need to hire boats to take them out there." The kids could see the wheels turning in the restaurant owner's head.

"The old people seemed kinda freaked out about it when we told them." Sam watched for a reaction from Mavis. "Not sure why they'd be worried about a bunch of snakes."

"Yeah, isn't it just the snake pits out there?" Chickadee asked no one in particular.

Mavis wriggled in her chair. The kids knew it always took her a while to pull up the good gossip. Something inside wanted to get out when she shifted around like that.

"That's why we wanted to find Gramps. We wanted to ask him if there's anything special out there." Sam knew Mavis loved to be the first to tell a secret.

Mavis took a drag of her smoke and leaned forward, although no one else was in the place, she spoke quietly, "'Kay, don't tell anyone I told you this…"

The two Muskrats looked at each other and smiled. This was how Mavis started her best gossip.

"Those old people, they want to keep everything secret. Why? Maybe the town could be making money off those secret places if they weren't afraid of letting people know where they are."

The kids nodded reassuringly, so she continued.

"But old Rabbit-man, back when he used to drink, came in here one night and talked about what he called The Refuge. I'm pretty sure he said it was out past the snake pits."

The Muskrats looked at each other, slightly surprised that there might be some truth to their speculation.

"I never asked the old people about it. They'd probably give ol' Rabbit-man heck, so I never did." She shrugged her shoulders.

"Well, that sounds like it might be something." Chickadee was already heading for the door in her mind. Mavis's phone-dialing finger was twitching.

"We still need to find our grandpa and tell him the news, so we better be going." Sam's chair screeched against the rough wood of the bare floor as he stood.

With hurried good-byes, the kids left the House-taurant. Mavis waved to them with phone in hand.

The kids began to walk in the direction of the Station.

"So, there *is* something important back there. Must be really special for the Elders to keep it from everybody… well, most people," Sam speculated out loud.

"Yeah, Grandpa didn't even tell us!" Chickadee sounded a little betrayed.

"Well…you know how he's always on about earning things…even knowledge. Maybe this is one of those things. Otter said he didn't even know about it…and he's really trying to learn."

"I'm trying to learn!" Chickadee's anger flashed.

Sam gave her a little punch. "C'mon cuz, you know you spend too much time on that computer."

"Okay, that's true. But things like this make me wish…"

"Yeah, I know, sometimes you don't know there's a deeper level."

★

It was getting dark by the time the kids got to the Station.

This was where the after-dinner crowd, the miners, gathered to talk about their day. It was usually just the working guys, but this time a table of the big bosses sat in the middle. Chickadee and Sam recognized Mr. Makowski, and from the glint in his eye, they could tell he recognized them, too. After a quick look around, the Muskrats went to leave.

"Hey, you kids!" Mr. Makowski bellowed across the room. All eyes turned to Sam and Chickadee. They turned to look at the man.

"I hear your uncle found a boat!"

"Yeah, it's the one the archeologist rented." Sam stepped in front of Chickadee.

"Well…where's the old man?" The manager's voice was filled with scorn. Sam knew the company man wouldn't speak to his uncle this way.

"My uncle will find him, if anyone can. He's a great tracker."

"Tracker!?" Makowski chortled. "Well, that *tracker* needs to get his idiot niece off my pier." His voice dripped with anger.

After a pause, the kids turned to leave.

"I wasn't finished talking to you!"

Sam and his cousin turned back. They wanted to ignore the man but respecting their Elders was ingrained.

Mr. Makowski spoke with a sneer. "I know that Pixton was excited about something. It had nothing to do with the mine. I don't think so, anyway. He enjoyed his craft. Enjoys…"

He shook his head. "I know those traditionalists would rather sit in the Stone Age than evolve. I wouldn't be surprised if they got rid of that old man. Maybe they did it just to delay our work." He shrugged and looked around at the other company men. "Who knows? Bunch of savages around this place." Some of the men laughed, some didn't.

"You finished?" Sam glared at Makowski.

"You can go." The manager flicked his hand.

Sam and Chickadee left the Station.

Sam took his cousin home before he returned to his parents. They walked in silence and said quick good-byes.

Atim was already back home when Sam got there and filled him in on what had happened out in the bush.

CHAPTER 8

Searching Near the Snake Pits

As usual, Otter was the first out of the boat when they got to the rocky shore. With the boat's rope in hand, he pulled the bow on to the hard limestone edge so that the others could hop out. Uncle Levi handed Otter the dog's leash and took the tie rope. The shore rose steeply from the water and they had to scramble up an embankment to get fully on to solid land. The evergreens eked out a meager living on the thin layer of black soil that covered the pitted, sterile limestone underneath. Thick, spongy moss and tough bramble lived off the thin resources in the dirt and the little sunlight that pushed through the trees. It was this same dark soil that formed the mud of the delta.

The trio and the police dog had a large portion of the bay's arc to cover to get to the place closest to the stranded boat. Otter was already picking himself out a walking stick that could support his slight frame.

Atim assessed the shoreline and the difficulty of traversing it. "Are we going to walk along the shore here, Uncle?" he asked. "It might be easier if we took the trail to the snake pits and then cut in."

"We'll have to take the hard road. I want to be sure the dog gets a chance to whiff this whole stretch. Maybe, we'll walk out along that trail."

Atim shrugged, but he wasn't excited about trying to scramble over the steep shore between the bush and the water. His stomach growled.

"Here, big guy." A smirking Otter passed Atim a much thicker walking stick than his own. "This *might* keep you out of the water."

Atim flicked the hair out of his eyes and grabbed the stick with a mock show of anger. They both laughed.

"Boys," their uncle looked over at them with a touch of a smile, "quit being funny and come here."

He surveyed the trek they were about to take. "We have to find Dr. Pixton. This winter held on so long, the nights are still getting cold. Heck, we still had snow before the rain the other day. If he's out here cold and wet…"

He looked at them seriously and then shook his head. "I'm pretty sure even a city guy like him can last one night, but…not too much more…."

Out from the inside of his jacket, Uncle Levi brought a large Ziploc bag containing some crumbled cloth. He shouted out Scout's name.

"We paid a lot of money for this mutt to be trained, so he better work."

The dog came running over from a rotting tree stump he had been investigating and nuzzled up against their uncle's leg.

"Pixton's shirt," he announced as he pulled it from the bag and presented it to the German shepherd. The excited dog took great interest in the smells on the garment. "Hopefully, this will give him what he needs to find that old guy."

The dog continued to snuffle and snort at the shirt. Then Uncle Levi put the shirt back in the bag. "Search, Scout. Search."

The dog looked into his handler's eyes and then began to search the ground with his nose. He cast back and forth, but soon started going over old ground. He seemed unable to find what he was looking for.

"I don't know if he'll find any scent. If Pixton was out in the rain, the water may have washed it away." Their uncle looked off into the distance. "But hopefully, we'll find something." Uncle Levi grabbed an ax from the patrol boat and they started to walk along the edge of the bay.

Otter and Atim waded at the edge of the water, using the limestone shelf that stuck out from the shore. Their uncle walked on top of a man-high, limestone cliff covered in mud and brush. Scout swept back and forth over the ground, covering the distance between the walkers and more.

The going was tough. After a few minutes, their uncle called them up to him.

The boys waded out of the water and scrambled up the steep shore.

"How old?" Their uncle pointed at a pile of gray bear poop.

Otter studied the stool and its crumbling mass. What story did it tell? It had rained the day before yesterday. It was partially hidden by the foliage around it, but it was also on the edge of a windy lake.

"Six days?" Otter ventured.

"Good guess, I'd say." Their uncle shrugged and started walking again. After a few steps, he gave the dog another sniff at the shirt. The boys followed in his wake rather than returning to the cold water. Eventually, Atim took the ax from his uncle and led, hacking and cracking the foliage in front of him. Their uncle laughed at the amount of noise he was making. Atim tried to be quieter but it slowed them down. The tireless dog ran around them in circles, nose to the ground.

It took over two hours of hard work to get to the point on the bay that was closest to the abandoned boat. It wasn't far from where the stream left the tree line and pushed its load of silt into the delta. For eons, the cycle of rain had washed bits of black earth over the limestone base and into the stream. Across the muck of the delta, the RCMP patrol bobbed on the water. Atim waved at them in the distance. A handful of gulls floated in the air above the waves.

The dog loped back and forth, then ran out to where the stream met the bay.

"Nothing!" Their uncle threw his hands in the air.

Otter looked back along the stream. It would be easier to walk down the stream's bank. There was a lot less brush to wrestle through as the trees were restricted to outcroppings scattered on the exposed rock.

"The snake pits are not far down there." Atim flicked the hair from his eyes.

Uncle Levi was studying the stream. The boys looked at him and then each other. They knew their uncle was assessing how much work it would be to wade across.

"There's a bridge over the stream for tourists by the snake pits." Atim sounded hopeful.

Uncle Levi looked at the both of them and then back at the stream.

"Okay, we'll walk along the stream to the snake pits."

The boys sighed.

Uncle Levi brought out the shirt again and let the dog smell it. The bridge by the pits was a good half of a mile back from the lake. Otter was happy here, he liked the noisy "silence" of the bush, from the whispered rattle of the leaves, to the soft slither of the breeze. On the other hand, Atim wasn't so pleased. He liked the bush but hated dragging his large frame through it. He muttered his complaints quietly for fear of earning a look from their uncle. Children in their family were expected to carry their load with few complaints.

The snake pits were the closest thing the community had to a tourist attraction. When the government idea of hotels on First Nations swept through, the limestone had been crushed for a road leading off the highway, a parking lot, tourist dock, and trail. The pits still provided jobs to a few of the local kids every summer, but the anticipated hordes of tourists never made it past the many snake pits down south. Only those curious souls who traveled the highway stopped. Others came by boat and tied to the dock down by the parking lot. It was a much easier route then slogging through the bush along the bay.

Once out of the trees, it was easier to see into the distance.

"Look at the hawks." Uncle Levi pointed at two brown hawks hovering over the trees some distance away in the direction of the snake pits.

As they watched, Scout gave out a funny little whine and started to circle an area of the parking lot.

"Looks like he's stuck." Uncle Levi hitched up his belt. "That spot is kinda shaded from the rain. May be the only place he can pick something up."

The joy Scout had at finding what he was looking for

was evident. He pranced again and again in a tight circle. Eventually, Uncle Levi snapped on the leash and led the excited dog away.

A set of bathrooms stood along the trail down to the dock. When Uncle Levi led Scout inside, he gave out a funny whine before circling and leading them back toward the door. He huffed in frustration when the scent disappeared once they were outside.

"He was here." Their uncle looked at the boys. "But his scent isn't along the lake."

"Fish told us he took the old man to a few places," Otter said.

"Fish?" Their uncle shook his head. "How'd you find that out?"

"We're the Mighty Muskrats," Atim said. The boys smiled.

Their uncle laughed.

"Well...we may need to bring in more searchers. Someone pulled that boat in. If not the guy who rented it, then who?"

The boys shrugged.

"Let's head back into town."

CHAPTER 9

Learning Ancient Secrets

The next morning, the Mighty Muskrats were reunited at their grandfather's house. Chickadee and Sam were busy doing chores while Atim and Otter cut kindling and brought in the wood. As usual, Uncle Levi was there, sharing a morning tea with his father. The house held the fading smell of sweetgrass from Grandpa's morning prayers.

"Did you go see her?" Uncle Levi asked, looking out the big window over the fast-moving water outside. He was in almost the same clothes as the day before, his Windy Lake Police Service jacket, a T-shirt, and a pair of jeans with the shape of his wallet worn into the back pocket.

"No." Grandpa laughed. His old cowboy shirt, with its light green tartan, had been brighter many moons before. His jeans were ancient.

Chickadee and Sam looked at each other with a touch of surprise. They hadn't forgotten that Denice was still on the pier but had assumed their grandfather had at least taken her dinner or something.

"It was chilly last night." Uncle took a sip of his tea.

"She chose the time and location of her quest. I just want to see how serious she is."

"She's always serious. And stupid." Uncle grunted.

Grandfather leaned forward and looked back at the kids. "Chickadee, go bring me that old blanket, the green blanket, that nice one of your grandmother's. Samuel, bring me more tea."

Grandma had died almost five years before, but the house still looked as it did when she left it. The quilted green, white, and black star-blanket hadn't been used since she died. She called it her "good blanket" and saved it for special occasions.

Grandfather looked back out the window. The two men sat in silence for a while.

When Sam brought the tea, his grandfather's steady hand held out his cup. "When your uncle is finished his tea, we'll go see your cousin and bring her the blanket. Go tell the others."

Samuel lifted the teapot and met his uncle's eye.

Uncle Levi shook his head.

Sam knew he was being sent out of the room so his grandfather could say something private to his uncle. He wanted to know what was going to be said so much his teeth hurt.

When Chickadee returned from the guestroom with the blanket, Grandpa told her to put it in a garbage bag so it would be kept clean. Once it was in, Sam took the plump bag from his cousin and nodded toward the door.

As they were putting on their shoes, their grandfather began to speak to their uncle. "Your niece is fighting for her community...just like you are." Uncle Levi grunted but said nothing.

The door growled angrily as the two Muskrats left the house.

Chickadee and Sam giggled as they approached their cousins at the wood pile.

"We think Uncle Levi is getting heck from Grandpa." Chickadee laughed. Atim and Otter looked at each other, surprised.

"What? What for?" Atim shook his head.

"For calling Denice stupid, I think." Sam smiled as he shrugged.

"Not seeing her as a warrior, I think," Chickadee ventured.

Atim was about to speak when Grandpa's door squealed again. Uncle Levi stepped out and shut it behind him. He strode over to the kids.

"Grandpa's going to come out soon. I think he wants to take a package to Denice."

"Where are you going to look for the archeologist today, Uncle?" Samuel squinted against the midmorning sun.

"The RCMP are taking charge…." Their uncle paused for half a second. "Even though it's on rez land. We're taking volunteers to comb the bush by the bay. We'll start around the snake pits and move deeper in. If we have to…."

Uncle Levi look off down the road. "You kids can come with Mark later if you like."

"That sounds good," Sam said.

"We have to find Dr. Pixton. He's an Elder and it's chilly at night. We don't know if he has any fire or food," Uncle Levi said.

"Well, we'll try to do what we can," Chickadee assured him.

"Look after your cousin first." Uncle Levi nodded and turned. He gave a quick wave through the window as he drove away.

Grandpa came out of the house, his long walking stick in hand, and headed toward the company pier. Atim stuck the ax in the chopping block. When he caught up to Sam he took the big bag from his smaller brother. The Muskrats followed their Elder.

The sun was already hot enough that the dew had long since dried. The white gravel of road would soon be shedding dust. The birds in the trees on either side chattered noisily. A gentle but committed breeze pushed its way through the evergreens.

"What are we taking her, Grandpa?" Chickadee pulled up beside him. The old man had thrown on a well-worn, quilted-wool jacket and cowboy boots for the journey.

"Just your grandma's blanket." The old man paced his strides with the long stick, though he didn't seem to need it.

"No food?" Chickadee was concerned.

"She doesn't need food on a vision quest," Grandpa said.

Chickadee looked back at her cousins, wide-eyed. They shook their heads in surprise.

Sam caught up to Chickadee and his grandfather.

"Grandpa, what do you think of them searching by the snake pits?"

The Muskrats noticed their Elder stiffen a little, but he kept on walking.

"They won't find him there."

"Is there anything special there? Anything he would have been looking for…as a bone-digger?" Samuel probed.

Grandpa walked on in silence. The Muskrats held their breath.

"We heard a story about a secret hiding place there." Sam continued to look for answers. "But if you don't know anything about it…"

Grandpa stopped. His eyes flashed with anger as he looked at Samuel and then each of the Mighty Muskrats in turn. For an instant, a smile flickered across his face, but it was quickly lost in a grumble. He began to walk again. Grandpa's stick went *tock, tick, tock, tick* on the ground.

"If it's knowledge we have to earn, Grandpa..." Chickadee, a little worried, looked up into her Elder's face.

The old man's frown broke into a smile. "It would be hard to tell you kids there is nothing there if you've already seen the sign. And if you've already found and read the sign, then you've done much to earn new knowledge."

The Mighty Muskrats smiled. Chickadee and Atim blinked back tears. Otter and Samuel felt a rising warmth in their hearts. It was a great thing to earn a little more of their Elder's trust.

Their grandfather walked along quietly. The Muskrats knew he was collecting his thoughts. They were almost a quarter of a mile down the road before he began to speak again.

"Long ago, before the coming of the towns and cities, before the coming of the missionaries, before the coming of fur traders, our nation's history was taken up with our relations with the Dakota and Anishinaabe to the south and the Dene to the north." Grandpa nodded. It was a good place to start the story. "For many years the Dakota and Anishinaabe fought, but occasionally, they would come north to our lands. Sometimes it was an alliance between the two that allowed their warriors time to explore. Sometimes one side or the other suffered a great defeat and the winning warriors sought out other sources of glory. And the Dene, north of us, were always trying to come a little farther south, to share a little more of the warmth of our lands. Sometimes they came in desperation. Sometimes they came because their stomachs were full."

The old man motioned to a spot where a shelf of rock poked out of the brush. "I need to sit down to tell this story."

Chickadee took his hand and helped him across a dry, thin strip of high ground that led across the ditch. The skeletal rushes of last year rattled as they brushed by. The other kids followed.

When Grandpa was settled, he sat in silence for a while, catching his breath, and remembering ages past. Chickadee was beside him, watching him, holding his hand. Atim lowered himself behind them, hunched over the bagged blanket on his lap and looking off down the road. Standing with his hands in his pockets, Sam was trying to see how far he could peer into the bush. The thin spruce created a wall of gray. As he paced around the group, Otter studied the ground at his feet, picking up the occasional stone and throwing it across the road.

Eventually, Grandpa spoke again.

"In those times of war, our warriors needed a place to hide those most precious to them. A place that could protect us, when our enemies invaded our lands, but also in the harshest winters, when the winds and the snow became too much or stayed too long."

In the distance, the snap and crackle of a vehicle coming down the gravel road could be heard.

Grandpa motioned toward the south and the delta. "Back there, beyond the snake pits, is a cliff in the limestone, and against that soft rock, the water flowed. And over time it carved a great cavern. That is The Refuge. It is used, maybe once every four generations, but it has been kept a secret since time began for our people."

"If it's just a cave, why would the archeologist be excited about it?" Sam asked.

"The caches." Grandpa looked him in the eye. "For generations, especially in times of plenty, families have cached food in the area. Some used cracks in the rock, some used the deeper dirt above and behind The Refuge, but there are caches all over. Some of them are many generations old."

The dented rez truck speeding down the road was suddenly upon them...and then gone. Atim tossed the hair out of his eyes and waved as it went past. Then they were engulfed in a cloud of white dust that followed in the wake of the beaten vehicle.

Grandpa waved his hand in front of his face. The kids dramatically coughed and waved their arms. Atim and Otter bent over holding their tummies. They laughed when the cloud began to clear.

Grandpa asked if the blanket got dusty. Atim shook his head and held up the bag. Its opening was scrunched in his large fist. Static held the dust firmly to the outside of the once-shiny plastic bag.

Samuel coughed. "But wouldn't people use their caches? Wouldn't most be rotten?"

"Old and rotten is what archeologists make their money off of." Grandpa was annoyed by the dust. He wanted to walk again. Chickadee helped him slide off the rock and back onto his feet. Otter held on to Grandpa's walking stick so his Elder could use it to pull himself up.

Once moving, their grandfather started his explanation again. "And yes, sometimes the families went back and got their caches...sometimes they didn't. But it was a rule that you didn't touch anyone's stores except your own. Over so many generations, so many families...there is a lot of our people's work in the ground there."

"So, you think the company man might be back there?"

"I don't think so." Grandpa shook his head. "But if there is a big RCMP search in the area The Refuge may be found by outsiders."

"Why don't you think the archeologist is there, Grandpa?" Sam asked.

"Well, he could be. I don't *know*, but I don't feel it." Grandpa shrugged, unwilling to explain his intuition beyond that.

"Then how did the boat get there?" Sam challenged gently.

"I don't know. But boats float even without a man in them."

"What about the rope being pulled toward the shore?"

"I don't know about that one either…but the answer is out there. Go look again." Grandfather waved in the direction of the delta.

CHAPTER 10

Visiting a Water Warrior

The Mighty Muskrats and Grandpa turned off the road and onto a shortcut through the bush. It was dark, cool, and damp under the trees. Soon they were back on the road that led past the company pier.

At the gate, the old man explained why they were there. The company lot was busy. There was much hustle and bustle. The large trucks were leaving like clockwork.

The guards went through their grandfather's jacket and searched the blanket they had brought for Denice. Grandpa chuckled as the guards unfolded the blanket looking for something that wasn't there. Then he insisted they fold it up again. When they went to frisk Grandpa, his smile turned to a frown. But it was relit with a guffaw as the guard searched the old man's ticklish spots.

"We good?" Grandpa smiled at the young man who searched him.

Slightly chagrined, the guard nodded. "Sorry about that," he mumbled, not meeting the old man's eye.

The company man looked over the kids but didn't bother searching them. Instead, he led the five of them across the yard, around the warehouse, and down the pier. It was there an uncomfortable and dejected Denice sat.

"Grandpa!" The relief in her voice was obvious. "Did you bring any food?"

"No, my girl." Grandpa gave her a happy, proud smile. "But we brought you a blanket."

Their cousin had been leaning heavily against the post she was hugging. Her face was dirty, and her hair hung in wet strings. Chickadee quickly began rubbing her shoulders and back.

"Ho-lee, cousin," Otter said quietly.

"Grandpa! I'm so hungry...and cold," Denice said quietly.

"Well, take this, my girl." Grandpa motioned to Atim to take out the blanket. "This is your Grandmother's good blanket. I want you to take care of it while you're here."

Once it was out of the bag, Atim handed the star-blanket to his grandfather.

"Take care of it?! I'm sitting on a dock, Grandpa. I can't even use my arms. Look how dirty it is here."

"Well, you'll have to be careful." The old man spread the blanket over her back with Otter's help.

"I…I…" Denice looked down at the pattern covering her shoulders.

"You're hungry…" Grandpa took a seat on a nearby crate. A group of workmen walked past, curious at the little family gathering on their dock.

"So hungry, Grandpa. But you didn't bring any food!"

"I have some water." The old man unclipped a plastic bottle strapped to his belt. He gave it to Otter. The boy went over to his cousin and held it to her lips. Denice bowed her head and drank eagerly.

"Only a little!" Grandpa held up his hand, and Otter pulled the bottle away. Denice coughed and sputtered. Chickadee kneeled down and wiped her cousin's mouth with her sleeve. At that moment, the company manager rounded the corner of the warehouse with a group of men.

"Do you want to leave this place, child?" Grandpa asked. "It has been a cold night."

At this Denice sat up and shook the self-pity from her face. She flashed a determined smile.

"They'll destroy our water, Grandpa. They'll…you see what the hydro dam does to the shore." Denice was getting fired up even amidst her pain.

"All right, all right. We'll be going then." Grandpa got up to leave.

"Grandpa…why did you come if you're not going to bring food or help me?"

"We brought you a sip of water, which is more than some get on a quest." Grandpa smiled affectionately.

"Who are you? And what are you doing here? I didn't authorize your entry!" Mr. Makowski was not enraged like he had been the day before, but he was pretty stern nonetheless.

"I'm her grandfather." The old man hopped off the crate and walked to Denice.

"Well, if you didn't come to cut her loose, we don't want you here. We don't want anyone bringing her supplies." Mr. Makowski swung his arms as he spoke.

"I gave Denice her grandmother's blanket." Grandpa was slow and calm. When he was talking to someone who was angry, Grandpa always spoke to them as though they were children. It made him seem a little child-like himself, but only to those who didn't know him. "It is an old blanket, one of the last that my wife made before she passed. I hope you won't mind. We don't want her to get sick."

The manager scratched the back of his head. "Well... no...we don't want her getting sick...on my pier." His mind was working. "The blanket is all right. But nothing else." Mr. Makowski sounded resigned. "And I think it's time to leave..." he said sternly but taking care not to command the old man.

"Yes, I think it is time to go." Grandpa nodded in agreement. "We will be back for her, if not tomorrow... the next day. She'll have had her vision by then."

"The next day? I want her out of here today!"

Grandpa looked into the manager's eyes. "Oh, I don't think that will happen. She'll be fine here for another day...or two." He turned and laid a hand on Denice's head. He closed his eyes and said a little prayer.

"Okay...it's time to go, children."

Chickadee took the old man's elbow. His walking stick began to *tick, tock, tick* down the pier.

"I'll be back tomorrow evening, my girl," the old man shouted over his shoulder.

The Mighty Muskrats followed Grandpa back around the warehouse. Mr. Makowski and his men followed a little way behind them, making sure they actually left.

The gate clinked closed with a rattle.

With that task done, Grandpa was in the mood for tea. The Muskrats walked him to their Auntie Yvette's house for some bannock and a visit.

At the end of the driveway, the cousins paused, unsure of what direction to take down the gravel rez road.

"What do you want to do now?" Chickadee asked Sam.

"Well, Grandpa said he doesn't think the archeologist is where they're looking."

"Then how would the boat get there?" Atim picked up a rock and threw it over their aunt's house.

"It could drift, I suppose." Sam pinched his chin as he thought.

"Water's still high from winter melting." Otter stopped Atim from throwing an even bigger rock over the house.

"Let's go to the clubhouse." Samuel had figured out a plan.

"What's at the clubhouse?" Atim shook Otter's hand off his arm.

"There's something I want Chickadee to look up on the computer." Samuel smiled.

"Cool. Let's go!" Chickadee said and started running down the road. Her cousins looked at each other and then ran after her.

CHAPTER 11

Winter's Shadow

Once in the comfort of their secret place, the kids gravitated to their usual spots. Chickadee turned the computer on. Samuel went to his books, put his feet up on the dash, and opened his current read to the bookmark. Atim sat on his weight bench and picked up a barbell. He flicked the hair out of his eyes. Otter occupied his own chair and began to strum his guitar.

Once the computer was humming, Chickadee gave Sam's shoulder a push. "So, what do you want me to check out?"

"I don't know, really." Samuel sat up.

"What!?" Chickadee feigned anger.

"Well, I want to figure out how that boat could have got there. I figured there must be some kinda info on the Net about…I don't know."

"It was a long, snowy winter. The water is still high

from the snow melting," Otter stated as his fingers danced over the guitar strings.

"That would mean the water would sit higher on the delta." Atim grunted between lifts.

"Doesn't the mine's dam have its own website?" Samuel pinched his chin.

"Yeah." Chickadee's fingers started typing furiously. "I've checked it for Uncle Jacob before he's gone out fishing."

"He'd be good to have back. He's the best tracker in the family." Atim added weights to the leg press.

"Well…he's out in the bush. And I don't think he'd really be worried about some bone-digger!" Samuel chuckled. "What does the website say?"

"It says that the spillway was opened because of the spring runoff and the rainstorm the other night. They're calling it a 'rain-on-snow event.'"

"So, the water by the delta would be changing. It would have been high and then dropped." Sam was getting excited. "That could explain how it looked like the boat was pulled into the delta."

Atim stopped doing leg lifts and sat up. "Yeah. But what about the rope? It was pulled out like someone tried to drag the boat to shore. If it was pushed there by waves, the rope would be trailing out along the side."

"First things first. We'll solve that problem when we get to it," Sam assured Atim.

His brother mumbled, "We're there now."

Sam ignored him and went back to looking over Chickadee's shoulder. "What are you looking at now?"

She tucked a lock of her raven-black hair behind her ear as she studied the computer.

"I'm trying to figure out…if Dr. Pixton's boat was blown to the delta, where it was blown from." Chickadee leaned into her screen intently. "I'm looking back at the day of the storm on the weather website."

"Great idea." Sam patted her on the back.

Otter began to play a faster, happier song. His cousins laughed at the musical mood change.

"This website says the wind was blowing southeast that day." Chickadee smiled brightly as she found the information.

"Okay, that's wicked!" Sam jumped around the computer table. "Now, just go to that satellite map of the lake. Where would the boat be coming from?"

"The northwest shore, obviously," Chickadee scoffed. "But what's over there that an archeologist would be interested in? Here's the map."

The Mighty Muskrats gathered around the computer.

"There're the rock paintings." Atim pointed.

"And there's the old winter campsite." Sam slid his finger over the site and then pulled it back.

"What else is there?" Chickadee asked.

It was quiet in the fort as the kids studied the map.

"There's the sun dance grounds," Otter ventured.

"Yeah, I thought that too." Chickadee nodded.

"Me too," Atim said but then shook his head. "Why would an archeologist be interested in them?"

"They're sacred," Otter whispered.

"Yeah, but new sacred." Samuel pinched his chin. "Well…it's a place to start."

"Do you think this means Uncle Levi is searching the wrong side of the lake?" Otter crossed the bus and leaned his guitar against the opposite wall.

Chickadee turned from the computer and looked at him. "I don't know."

"Don't forget the boat rope!" Atim's voice was laced with frustration. "It was *stretched out*. It really looks like that boat was pulled in."

The cousins stood in silence for a moment.

"We could ask Fish if he took Pixton to the snake pits. If he did, then that would explain what the dog picked up."

"Okay," Atim gave up some ground, "but I think we need to figure out who pulled the boat in." Otter nodded in agreement.

"Well…I promise we'll figure that out before we go tell Uncle he's searching in the wrong place. 'Kay?" Samuel bargained.

Atim and Otter smiled. "Sounds good."

Sam smiled back.

Chickadee rolled her eyes and shook her head at the boys. "Well...now that we've decided that, let's go find Fish again and ask him if he ever took Dr. Pixton to the snake pits."

She laughed again when her cousins all nodded their heads in unison.

CHAPTER 12

A Different Perspective

The Muskrats figured they'd try the gas station before they went anywhere else. As they came out of the bush trail, they could see a bunch of the company men standing in the parking lot with the RCMP and the band constables.

"Where the heck are all your people?" Mr. Makowski was agitated again.

"We put out a call for volunteers. I'm not from around here." The senior RCMP officer shrugged.

"When is that Makowski guy not angry?" Atim wondered.

"Everyone wants to be boss, but he sure makes it seem like more of a hassle than it's worth." Chickadee shook her head.

The RCMP officer spoke to their uncle. "Did you put out the call to your people?"

Uncle Levi sighed and nodded.

Makowski turned his ire on the local police officer.

"You're supposed to be the authority in this town. Where are all your people?"

Uncle Levi looked around the empty parking lot. "I don't know where they are." He shrugged. "But it is a volunteer position."

"Well, it's not like any of them are working! Where are they?" The manager swept his arm over the whole town.

Their uncle sighed again. "How many of your men are volunteers? Or are they getting paid?" Uncle Levi quietly looked him in the eye.

The manager glared at the police officer but didn't say anything. The employees quietly smiled. Apparently, they were being paid to be there.

With a smirk, Uncle Levi suggested, "We can do a lot with what's here. There may be more tomorrow."

Mr. Makowski took the edge off his anger. "There's an old man out there. He isn't going to last long."

Uncle Levi agreed. "I know it. That's why I'm here. Now, we're going to head out to the snake pits and walk through the bush to see if we can find him. There are few hours of daylight left, so I suggest we get moving."

"This bloody community doesn't care about an old man?" Mr. Makowski shook his head.

Uncle Levi was on his way to the truck, but he answered with his deep voice, "He's your old man. Why didn't you know him well enough to take care of him?"

Uncle Levi didn't wait for a response but took the last two steps to his truck and got inside. He rolled down the window and looked at Makowski sternly. "I'll meet you and your men at the snake pits in about two hours."

"We'll be there." Mr. Makowski nodded and headed back to his vehicle.

With the manager on his way, Uncle Levi motioned to the kids.

"What's up, Uncle?" Chickadee skipped up to his window. The other Mighty Muskrats followed.

"We're heading down to the snake pits to search. Do any of you want to come?" The Muskrats looked at each other and then back at their uncle.

"I think we're following other leads..." Samuel squinted at his uncle.

"Other leads, hey?" Uncle Levi nodded thoughtfully. "Well, I have to follow the only lead I have. The RCMP seem to be leading the charge on this. But...if you guys come up with anything you let me know."

"We will, Uncle," Sam assured his Elder.

"Okay." Uncle Levi was serious but gave the kids a smile. "And if you can figure out why nobody showed up to search, let me know that, too. I bet your grandfather and the Elders may have something to do with it."

"No problem!" Atim said.

Their uncle grinned again, put his truck in gear, and drove off.

"What do we do now?" Atim wondered aloud.

The Mighty Muskrats decided to check out the Station as they hadn't found Fish yet.

The restaurant was slowly filling up as it got closer to the dinner hour. The waitress at the front asked them if they wanted a table. Sam had a little crush on her. He mumbled shyly, "We're just looking for Fish."

"Well, he ain't in my section." She slid the till shut and walked away. But as she left she flung out an arm in the direction of the dining room. "Go take a look if you want."

In a cluster, the Mighty Muskrats shuffled in. It didn't take long to confirm that Fish wasn't there.

As they turned to leave, a stranger spoke behind them in a gruff voice. "Hey, is it your cousin tied to the company dock?"

The cousins tightened up. They were expecting another blast from a mine employee. Atim puffed out his chest and Chickadee's face turned into a scowl. Otter waited to see what was going to happen.

They turned to look as one.

The young First Nation man's coveralls were full of dust and his face was dirty. His long hair was matted on top from sweating under the hard hat that now sat on the table.

With a touch of suspicion in his voice, Samuel said, "Yes, it is."

"She's a smart chick," he shook his head, "but not too smart."

When he saw the effect his last words had on the Muskrats he quickly held up his hands. "No, no. I like her! She reminds me of my sister. My sister back in Smokey Bend."

"Okay." Sam waited. Smokey Bend was a First Nation about a two-hour drive away. The Muskrats had been told that Smokey and their community were part of the same nation. A number of communities had traced their families back to a large group that once followed the same holy man, but that had been before they were herded onto the reserve. Smokey Bend was also where the long-distance Windy Lake Winter Festival Dog Sled Race turned around and headed back to Windy Lake.

"I sat with her during my coffee breaks today. Gave her some water, but she wanted food. We talked about a lot of stuff."

Suddenly realizing the Muskrats were standing in the middle of a busy room, he kicked out the chair across from him.

"Sit down," he said. "I'm saving the table for my buddies, but they won't be here for a while."

Sam looked at his brother and cousins. They shrugged, so he cautiously sat down. Chickadee took the other seat beside him. Atim and Otter just stood behind them.

"So, she was okay when you left?" Chickadee looked worried.

"She's pretty tough." The young man chuckled.

"I seen her hit an old boyfriend with a frying pan." Chickadee giggled.

"I could believe that," he said. "She got me to fold up her grandma's blanket and put it back in the plastic bag. Said she didn't want to get it dirty. She'd rather be cold. But yeah, I figure she'll be done tomorrow."

"What did you talk about?" Sam was curious as to why his cousin was interested in this company man.

"I told her I need my job. I got kids. I'm a single dad. My kids have school, so they're with my mom when I'm here, and then I get to hang out with them for the week I'm off. That kinda sucks sometimes, but…I need my job."

"She says the company is poisoning the water," Otter said from behind Sam.

"Believe me," he said. "She mentioned it to me, too."

He grew serious before he went on. "I told her, there's definitely stuff I see that I don't agree with. No doubt. But there are rules. And, I know, most of the managers make their guys follow them."

"Yeah, but money makes the world go 'round," Sam said.

"That's why a guy needs a job. World ain't perfect. I have to make something out of what I got…for who I got. That's how I'm supposed to be a good man, right?" The young man seemed to be honestly asking Samuel for his opinion.

Sam nodded. "That's what my grandpa says."

"I don't have the answers." The single dad shook his head. "All I have is these." Two dirty hands stretched out across the table.

Just then, a group of loud young men burst through the restaurant door. They were dressed in dirty overalls and hard hats.

"My buddies are here. But I'll make sure to give your cousin some water when I'm back at work tomorrow." He smiled at the Muskrats.

As Samuel rose to leave he asked, "What's your name?"

"My parents are Jacob and Rene Cardinal from Smokey Bend. I'm Steven." He held out his hand as his compatriots surrounded the table. Sam shook it and said good-bye.

CHAPTER 13

Rough Side of the Rez

"Seems like a nice guy," Atim said as the Mighty Muskrats left the Station.

"Yeah, I could see Denice liking him." Chickadee smiled.

"Wooooo-hoooo!" her boy cousins shouted as one. It ended in giggles.

"Sounds like little Chickadee has a crush!" Atim teased. Chickadee punched him in the gut. He gasped as the air quickly left his lungs.

"Let's go." Chickadee stomped off across the parking lot. Her cousins caught up to her once Atim could breathe.

"We still haven't found Fish…." Sam let the idea hang.

"Maybe we should stop and talk to Grandpa too." Chickadee still had a touch of annoyance in her voice.

"Yeah, I think that's a good idea." Sam pinched his chin as he thought.

"Back to the House-taurant?" Atim suggested cautiously.

"I bet Grandpa is already back home by now. Mavis really wanted to help get people out to search. I wonder what happened," Sam said out loud.

"Do you think the Elders had something to do with it?" As Chickadee stopped walking, the boys turned to look at her.

"That's why we want to talk to Grandpa, isn't it?" Sam said.

They all nodded.

"Fish's house is not far," Otter offered.

"But do we want to go there?" Chickadee asked with a touch of worry in her voice. It was well-known that a lot of the fights and crime in town were committed by only a few people and a number of those people were Fish's brothers and cousins. The corner of town where Fish and his cousins lived had become a tough neighborhood. The Muskrats tried to avoid it.

"It's nothing!" Atim's bravado spoke. He flipped the hair out of his eyes.

"Well…we better go quick. It'll be dark soon," Sam assured Chickadee. Otter took her brown hand in his own.

"Let's go." Chickadee started walking. Her freckled expression was determined with a dash of worry thrown in.

The Mighty Muskrats marched in silence to Fish's house.

As the houses on the reserve spread out over the folds and hills of an ancient lake bed, there were low points and high points. The homes had been built to government plans, erected by the lowest bidders. Some were crumbling with age; others could use a good coat of paint. Since there wasn't enough housing for the growing number of families on the rez, people stayed in buildings that would have been condemned in other places.

The road rose a little before it headed down into a small valley. Fish's house was one of the few clustered above the swampy soil that collected rain from the higher ground around it. The wet little depression always smelled of rotting weeds and wood. The bulrushes had escaped from the confines of the roadside ditches and consorted with willows and swamp grass in little tufts here and there.

The gravel on the road crunched as the Mighty Muskrats walked determinedly to collect a new bit of information.

Sam whispered, "Okay. We just want to know if Fish ever took the doctor to the snake pits."

"What if he's not home?" Atim tried to sound casual.

"Then we just came for a nice walk!" Otter smiled at his cousins.

Fish's yard was so muddy that the trucks were parked along the side of the gravel road rather than the driveway. A tricycle, a go-cart, and a whole bunch of homemade, wooden toys were scattered across the mud and lawn.

Fish's house was a rectangle of aged plywood. The paint had long since faded. All that stood out from the gray of weathered wood was the faded pink insulation held in place over broken windows by wind-ripped, plastic sheeting.

The front step was an overturned fisherman's box. Atim didn't bother to test it, he reached up and knocked on a corner of the screen door. Immediately, the sound of movement came from within. A lot of people seemed to be moving toward the door.

Atim stepped behind Samuel when the door swung open.

"Hey." A large, brown lady smiled pleasantly down at them. Fish's wife was from a much better family, and much to their chagrin, she had fallen in love with him back in high school. With the door open, a number of small children tumbled out, giggling and happy. A toddler clung to Mrs. Fish's leg.

"Uhm…we're here to talk to Fish." Sam was thankful she had answered the door.

"How's your cousin?" Mrs. Fish looked at Chickadee. She saw the Muskrats as a connection to others in their family.

"Which one?" Sam's forehead furrowed. His grandma had twelve kids. Some of his uncles and aunties had eight or more.

"Denice is okay, but she probably won't last past tomorrow." Chickadee knew that Mrs. Fish and her protesting cousin had gone to high school together.

"She was always crazy." Mrs. Fish chuckled. "But smart though. Glad she's doing what she's doing."

"Is Fish here?" Sam squinted up at her.

Mrs. Fish gave him the once over.

"This your cousin?" She looked at Chickadee.

"Yep." Chickadee surveyed Sam. "He moved here last year." She lip-pointed to Atim. "Him and his brother."

Mrs. Fish looked at Sam. "He's not here, city boy. What do you want him for?"

Sam suddenly felt self-conscious. "We're looking for a lost old man."

"The doctor, hey?" She picked up the toddler and placed him on her hip. The little boy was pleased to look down on their guests. Chickadee reached up and stuck her finger in his tiny hand and made baby noises at him.

Sam nodded.

"What about him?"

"Did Fish take him to the snake pits?" Sam's chagrin disappeared with the possibility of nailing down some information.

Mrs. Fish looked off in the distance, thinking. The sun wasn't far from the horizon. The clouds would soon start to change colors. "I think he did. I think it was the day before the storm. Took him to a bunch of places, the old winter site, the sun dance site and…I'm pretty sure the snake pits."

The Mighty Muskrats smiled at each other.

"Well, thank you." Sam smiled at Mrs. Fish.

She smiled back. "Well…at least you're polite. Kinda cute."

His cousins and brother laughed. Atim pushed his shoulder.

"We better be on our way." Chickadee waved at Mrs. Fish.

"Okay, see you around." Mrs. Fish nodded at them as she shut the door.

The freed children were busy playing in the front yard. Mud was smeared across their legs, arms, and faces. The Muskrats said good-byes to them as they left the yard. Atim pushed a kid on the tricycle for a quick dash. The little boy raised his feet off the spinning pedals and squealed at the speed.

With smiles on their faces, the Mighty Muskrats made their way out of the swampy little valley.

"We can tell Uncle that Scout probably picked up the doctor's scent from when he went there with Fish," Sam said.

"So maybe they'll stop searching there and look across the lake!" Otter said enthusiastically.

"Yeah, but what about the rope?" Atim was ready to remind everyone about the promise Sam made in the fort.

"We'll figure out the rope," Sam assured him.

"Let's go talk to Grandpa again, before we go home," Chickadee suggested as she skipped sideways down the road. Her cousins picked up their pace. The sun was now turning the clouds into pink and purple cotton candy in the distance.

★

As the House-taurant came into view, Atim began to think of reasons to go inside.

"We should go see what Mavis has for leftovers. She might give us some cold fries…if she has any."

"I thought we were going to talk to Grandpa. It'll get dark soon," Otter complained.

Atim decided to work on his brother.

"Fish's wife says she figured he went there, but that isn't for certain." He shrugged at his brother. "And we don't really know why no volunteers showed today to look for the old…Dr. Pixton."

Samuel pinched his chin as they walked. Chickadee noticed and rolled her eyes.

Resigned, Otter shook his head. "We can only stay for a while. Sun's going down," he insisted.

Samuel pointed down the road. "The House-taurant it is."

The door opened with a tinkle as the Mighty Muskrats filed into the home business.

"Hey, kids." Mavis was just going around the wall that hid the kitchen. Four of the tables in her living room had two or more guests at them. Atim lip-pointed to an empty table just inside the old dining room.

"How much money we got?" Chickadee nodded at the boys. Her cousins produced what little change and few bills they had. "Wow! Five dollars and sixty-five cents! What does that get us?"

Atim grabbed the menu. "I could get a burger and you guys could share the fries." He smiled. Otter gave him an elbow to the upper arm.

"'Kay, brother, that ain't happenin'!" Samuel snatched the menu out of his brother's hands. "We could get a large fries with gravy and two Cokes." The others nodded as Mavis approached the table.

"What do you guys want?" She was in her busy mode. The end of her pen hovered over a pad of paper.

"Fries and gravy, two Cokes, four forks." Chickadee took the menu from Sam and handed it to Mavis.

"Mm-hmmm." Mavis stuck the menu under her thick arm. She jotted down the order and took off toward the kitchen.

"Shoot! I want to talk to her." Sam half-stood and looked over the rest of the crowd. From one of the other tables, an old friend of his family's smiled at him with a gap-filled grin. Samuel nodded back and sat down.

"Don't worry about it. She'll be back." Chickadee smiled at Atim and Otter. They often teased Samuel for his lack of patience. His cousins were convinced it was something that he had caught, like a virus, in the city. Atim seemed to fit into the rez a little better.

"I just want to know what happened to the volunteers."

"The Elders must have said something," Otter said to his cousins.

Eventually, Mavis brought the fries to the table along with two Cokes and four forks.

Samuel was afraid he wouldn't get a chance to speak to her again.

He blurted out, "What happened to the volunteers?"

Mavis snorted. "You tell me. I told Ruth, Ester, Snippy, Pea-Soup, and Rolls. They were all into it and then Rolls called and said her grandma told her not to go. That was that. I didn't even hear back from the others...and they all have boats that could take people out. They wanted to help when I first told them."

Samuel was processing the information.

Mavis continued. "If you ask me, it was those Elders. Who knows where it started?" She threw up her hands. "But somebody says 'remember when' and then none of them move." She shook her head in disgust.

Sam nodded.

Chickadee rolled her eyes at his silence. "We don't know what happened," she explained to Mavis. "We were in the parking lot at the Station when the RCMP met the company guys. The big hothead manager was mad that there were no volunteers."

"Who? Makowski? I could tell you a few things about that guy." She chuckled, then remembered she was talking to the nosiest children in town.

She got serious. "If you want to know why the volunteers dried up...well, go and ask your grandfather. He's their...whatever you call it." Mavis dismissed the subject with a wave of her hand and then walked away.

CHAPTER 14

Searching for a Sign

It was still dark when Otter woke. He quietly snuck out of the house and into his grandfather's shed. When he came out he was lugging a small boat engine that weighed almost as much as he did. He loaded the engine into an old, tin wagon and pulled it down to the riverbank. The lake was almost wave free. A steady but shallow undulation reflected the night sky and the lights along the shore. The water lapping against the sand and stones was hardly louder than a whisper.

His grandfather's canoe was overturned on the shore. Otter pulled a life jacket out from under the canoe and put it on.

It wasn't long before Otter was gliding through the waves at the small engine's top speed. Its steady burp seemed to float out over the darkness of the lake. Otter's mind still rang with the words that his grandfather had spoken the night before.

★

The cousins had tumbled into Grandpa's just as the old man was putting on tea.

"You kids…help me clean up this place. I have guests arriving tomorrow," Grandpa directed them as soon as they walked in the door.

Chickadee went to the sink, turned on the hot water, and started organizing the few dirty dishes on the counter. Otter picked up the broom and started sweeping by the wood box and stove. Samuel lined up the boots by the door, organized the jackets, and put away the winter mitts, toques, and scarves. Atim left to get an armful of firewood.

Grandpa went out to the freezer in the shed and brought back a hunk of moose leg. Taking a big roaster from a cupboard he stood the haunch up inside and started to shave off slices of meat.

"I have some old friends on their way. They'll be here to honor the end of Denice's vision quest." Their grandfather smiled proudly to himself, but Chickadee, still washing dishes, noticed.

"We spoke to a guy from outta town who talked to her this afternoon," Chickadee said quietly. Grandpa looked over, his face held a shadow of worry. "He works for the company, but he's from Smokey Bend. He seemed like a nice guy."

The old man listened but carried on with his work.

Chickadee continued. "We saw him at the Station. He called us over. He told her that he needs his job. That he's a dad with kids. He…wanted the company to follow the rules, but…they didn't always. Still…he needed his job so he could give his kids a good life."

Grandpa continued to slice the meat. Finally, he laughed and said, "Maybe that will be her vision. We will see what comes of that."

Their Elder didn't say anything for a long time. Sam finished cleaning up in the entranceway and went to hold the dustpan for Otter.

Eventually, Grandpa held up the knife he was using to cut the meat, showing it to the kids.

"It's an old question, what would you rather go through life with, a knife or a hammer? Maybe that will be your cousin's vision."

The door squeaked open. Wearing his dirty outside boots, Atim walked over the recently swept floor and dumped a crumbling load of logs into the wood box. He immediately turned, kicked his boots sailing back into the entranceway, and then brushed the wood chips onto the kitchen floor.

The family looked at him.

"Were you guys talking about me, or what?" he asked when he noticed.

Chickadee returned to washing dishes. Grandpa

continued to slice the moose. Sam and Otter shook their heads and picked up the broom and dustpan again.

"What…?" Atim looked around confused.

Sam took the moment to change the topic of the conversation back to the Pixton case.

"You were right, Grandpa," Samuel said as he picked the larger wood chips up off the floor. "The boat may have floated on its own. The combination of the rainstorm on the snow caused a lot of water to pour into the lake…."

"So, the wind could have pushed it to the delta," Grandpa finished the thought. Chickadee nodded and smiled at him.

"The wind probably did push the boat," Chickadee said.

"But the shore rope was pulled out like someone tried to drag it." Atim retrieved a sock that had flown across the room when he kicked off his rubber boots. "We have to figure out what caused that…" Atim tossed the hair out of his eyes and looked at his brother, "…before we go to Uncle Levi." His voice was insistent.

"Yes, that's the sticky bit," Samuel said with a sigh.

Sensing the tension, Grandpa looked at the brothers. "You need to know who pulled the rope out?"

The Mighty Muskrats nodded. Grandpa went back to slicing his meat.

The kids knew he was thinking, so they continued with their chores quietly.

Their Elder eventually spoke. "Our people believe you are the land you live on. That means the land…the food that's on it—that which can be gathered and that which can be hunted—its seasons, its water…its possibilities, and even the very shape of the landscape pour themselves into the beings and spirits that live on it."

With the roaster full of meat, Grandpa put the cover on and placed it in the fridge. He picked up what was left of the haunch and motioned to Atim. "Go put this back in the freezer."

Atim gingerly, but quickly, took the still-frozen hunk of meat and bone and ran to the shed and back. While he was gone, the old man quietly washed his hands in the sink. When he was done, he put the kettle on and sat at the scarred wood table.

When Atim returned, Grandpa spoke again. "So, if you want to know a place, you must know the land. Know how it affects the animals and how they live their lives."

"Well, hopefully, a little bird will tell us." Sam shook his head. He had wanted to hear something more helpful from his Elder. His grandfather noticed his slightly hidden sarcasm.

"If you could talk to the birds, this mystery would already be solved," Grandpa chided. "Do you know what the birds know?"

Sam shook his head angrily.

★

The lake was so calm it mirrored the sky perfectly. The small engine on the canoe was slow but sincere as it pushed the craft through the crisp water. The trip seemed to take twice as long as on Uncle Saul's boat. Otter had passed the cultural camp an hour earlier, had watched the slow approach of the dock at the snake pits, and was now approaching the long, last point of land before the delta.

He didn't want to scare off anything in the bay, so he turned off the small motor. Leaning forward, he grabbed a paddle, but just held it crosswise across the canoe. Silently, he passed the fingertip of land and slipped into the crescent shape of Snake Creek Bay.

The point was covered in gray-trunked evergreens. They stood close together near the shore, creating a thin stretch of thick forest that hid the parking lot and buildings of the snake pits.

The thin sticks of spruce stopped short before a narrow stretch of field that gradually gave way to swamp grass as the land neared the water. Through it all, an occasional knee of limestone stuck out from the soil like a petrified whale caught in mid-breach.

The center of the bay was filled with the mud of the delta. Tufts of swamp grass indicated a smattering of small and medium islands within the fan of creeks, silt, and swamp. Willows sprouted in those areas dry enough to support roots. Bulrushes embroidered the edge of any standing water, and a pudding of black and gray mud fertilized the lot. For most of the year, Snake Creek was just a series of trickling fingers into the bay. The boat had been caught near the largest of these, where the water circulation kept the mud clean of foliage.

Otter floated along with the boat's momentum. A whispered breeze and the waves set his course. He looked down into the emerald-green water. The sun was taking a greater interest in making the waves sparkle as it climbed in the sky. It was going to be a warm spring day.

Otter was far enough from shore that most of the mosquitoes hadn't noticed he was near. For a long time he listened. The slightest shift in his weight relayed itself to the canoe. The motion of the craft was timed by the gently rolling waves. Otter tried to keep still. He sent his hearing out over the water. Far off, a gull complained. From deep inshore, a hawk warned its prey. With the rising temperature, the wind was slowly waking up. The bulrushes rustled somewhere along the shore.

He picked up the paddle and gently cut the surface of the water. The stringy sinews of his arm and shoulder pulled back. The paddle thunked against the canoe in its journey, and the watercraft lurched forward with each strong stroke.

Otter came to the place where the doctor's boat had become stuck in the mud. The mark of the boat's landing had long been lost as the mucky shore returned to its natural shape.

Otter watched the shore for a long time. His back began to ache with the effort of staying still in the light canoe.

Still, he stayed.

An uncle had once said to stay until you felt uncomfortable and then stay two times longer than that. Otter took a deep breath. The inhalation stretched out his back and rib cage. The water slapped against the side of the boat. After a few minutes, a large fly whizzed by.

The wind was slowly picking up. Otter continued to watch and listen and breathe. Far in the distance, he heard another screech. He searched the sky. High over the gray-green forest a raptor hovered in the air. It was too far away for even Otter's sharp eyes to make out more than its shape. He recalled his Grandpa saying "Do you know what the birds know?"

With that admonition to Samuel in his mind, Otter began to paddle toward the bird.

As he traveled, Otter's perspective on the land changed. He was better able to see that the bird hovered over the snake pits. He pulled in his paddle and coasted as he weighed his options. Returning to the dock at the snake pits would be easier than trying to walk from the closest point on the shore. Otter put his back into the next stroke.

As he passed the point, he kept an eye on the bird.

With a quick flick, Otter turned the canoe toward the dock. The light canoe cut through the water with each pull on the paddle. With fifteen minutes of hard work, he was gliding up to a little man-made beach beside the snake pits dock.

Gingerly, he stepped into the cold water. He was happy to be out of the canoe. His stomach muscles and shoulders were sore from the journey. Otter pulled the boat up onto the sand. He thought about the rising water that must have lifted Dr. Pixton's rental boat off whatever shore he was on and begun its trip to the delta. He looked over the lake and felt the strong wind on his face. That, too, had played its part. The final clue must be here.

From here the trees blocked the view of the hawk. He would have to go farther in to learn what the birds know.

CHAPTER 15

Vision Crunch

"He was gone when I woke this morning." Grandpa looked over his shoulder at Atim, Chickadee, and Sam. He turned back to look through the window at the lake. The remaining Muskrats stood in the entranceway, unsure of what to do next. With a gesture, Grandpa indicated a piece of paper on the table. "He said he was taking my canoe."

Chickadee picked up the paper, read it, and then showed it to the brothers. It said, "Grandpa, I'm taking the canoe. Otter"

Sam chuckled. "That sounds just like Otter."

Chickadee and Atim smiled. They teased Otter sometimes about his quiet ways. But when it came down to it, Otter didn't have to say much to be understood by his cousins.

"Do you think he went out to the delta?" Chickadee asked.

"By himself?" Atim sounded more disappointed than concerned.

"It's not much of a trip…for Otter." Sam had a lot of confidence in his cousin's ability to take care of himself.

"Don't worry about him." Grandpa had been listening. "You should be more worried about your other cousin, Denice."

"Yes! Denice!" Chickadee had almost forgotten their older cousin.

"Now is a very important time in her quest." Grandpa stared out the window again. "She can't end it too soon, or she will regret not embracing the challenge, once it's done. She can't stay in the wilderness for too long either, or it could harm her."

"She's just sitting on the dock right over there, Grandpa," Atim protested.

"Have you ever gone three nights without food and only a little water?" Grandpa look sideways at his grandson. "Your body calls…so harsh. Do you know what it does to your heart? Your mind? She is both weak and strong at this time."

Atim was appropriately chagrined. He looked at the floor.

"Your stomach aches so much that it feels like a hole in your soul." Grandpa was remembering days gone by. "There's a time when the thirst is so strong, you feel you'll do anything for a drink of water…but still you must sit…

to prove that you have command over those desires. That you are beyond the needs of your body."

"But I thought it was about finding your place in the community." Chickadee was always curious about her people's traditions.

"It is…. Once you see the world beyond your needs, it becomes easier to see your dreams and how you can contribute. But there's always the chance anger and the physical trial will beat you down. And you'll slide back…." Grandpa got up from his chair with a grunt and moseyed over to the fridge. "It's on that knife's edge where your cousin sits now." He opened the dented and chipped white door and took out a plastic bag tied with a knot on top.

"Take this to your cousin." Grandpa gave the care bag to Samuel.

"What do we say to her? She's going to ask for you," Sam said as he felt the weight of the bag and tried to guess what was inside. He felt the slosh and shape of a bottle, but it was far from full. The small, hard square could have been a handful of crackers. He gave the package to Atim.

"Tell her…tell her I sent this. Tell her I'm praying for her."

"What if she asks why you didn't come?" Chickadee knew her cousin would want to see her Elder.

"Tell her I know she has all she needs. And I will sing a song for her this evening to get her through the hard times."

"You'll go there?" Sam sounded unsure.

"No. I'll sing my song from home. This is still her quest."

Chickadee and Sam looked at each other. They knew Denice would be very disappointed.

"We'll make sure she gets it." Atim was eager to please after his reprimand.

Grandpa looked over his shoulder again as they started to leave. "Come back here later. My guests will be arriving this afternoon. I may need some chores done."

The kids assured him they would return and then said their good-byes.

Once the trio was outside and walking down the short white gravel driveway, Samuel threw his hand in the air. "Why did Otter go off alone?! Now if he finds something, we won't know about it until he gets back."

Chickadee laughed at her cousin. "You know he'll find something. You just can't stand to wait."

Atim giggled. "Yeah, you just need to plug the info in that thing on your shoulders."

Samuel smiled. "This is the information age! I got places to go, people to see."

Chickadee guffawed. "You leaving the rez?"

All three burst out laughing.

"'Kay, so how are we going to work on the case in the meantime?" Samuel was pinching his chin.

"Let's worry about Denice right now." Chickadee's concern was evident in her voice. "I can't imagine what it's like to be surrounded by those miners. They probably hate her."

Atim nodded. "I bet."

"Let's hurry!" Chickadee started jogging down the road. Her cousins picked up their pace.

Eventually they rounded the last corner that blocked their view of the company gate. They slowed to a walk.

"Do you think they'll let us in?" Atim flicked his hair while looking at the guards at the gate. There were fewer now that the entrance was no longer blocked by protestors.

"I wonder where Denice's friends are?" Chickadee's brow furrowed.

"Maybe they're like Gramps and figure this is her ordeal." Sam shrugged.

Chickadee looked thoughtful. "Maybe that nice guy from Smokey Bend who spoke to Denice earlier will be here."

They stopped in front of the gate, a little nervous about approaching the company men.

A large blond security guard with a big beard noticed them. He walked out of the compound and over to the kids. "Are you here for Denice?" He looked the three over.

The Mighty Muskrats were surprised that one of the miners knew their cousin by name.

"Yeah." Sam squinted up at the man.

"She's not looking good. Your family needs to get her out of here." The man sounded worried, not angry.

"We brought her something from our grandpa." Atim held up the package.

"Well…some of her friends were here earlier, but Makowski sent them packing." The man was struggling with the idea of letting them in. "They were protestors though…you're family."

"You could take it to her," Atim ventured.

Chickadee gave him a look that shut him up.

"Nooo…. Makowski might kill me for that." The man chuckled and shook his head. "She's a tough chick. A few of the guys were talking to her. At first, we thought she was crazy, but you know, she's just trying to protect her land."

The children were even more surprised by the miner.

"My auntie says because of the law First Nations live under, the environmental standards are less strict." Sam tried to sound adult.

"I don't know about that." The big guy shook his beard and looked over at the company building. It seemed he was trying to look through it at Denice. "I'm going to let you guys in. But you have to make it quick. Makowski is off the compound, but I don't know when he's coming back."

"Thanks. We just need to deliver this package and give her a message from our grandpa." Sam nodded at the man.

"Well, if anyone asks, tell them you climbed the fence." The blond miner laughed. "Get going! Make it quick!" He opened the compound gate.

The three kids took off across the yard. It didn't take long to get around the other side of the long warehouse and office.

Chickadee gasped when she saw her cousin. "Oh, Denice!" she cried as tears began to flow. The boys were speechless.

Denice leaned heavily against the pillar she was wrapped around. Creosote stuck to her arms, chin, and cheeks. Blobs of the tar clung to her long, black hair. Her eyes were dull.

"Water?" Denice looked up. Her neck seemed to struggle with the weight of her head.

Sam realized it was the first time he hadn't seen Denice smile when they met. He noticed her skin near the pipe that hid her hands had turned raw.

Atim had forgotten about the package, but he finally ripped it open and looked inside. A small, much-used bottle was about a quarter filled with cloudy water. Sediment of some kind was clinging to the bottom.

"Grandpa gave you this...to drink." He held up the bottle for everyone to see.

"Pour it in." Denice managed a smile. Atim gave the bottle to Chickadee. She was kneeling beside their older cousin, rubbing her shoulders, arms, and back. Chickadee carefully gave Denice a sip. She didn't want to spill any as there wasn't much. Denice tried to slurp it all up. But Chickadee pulled the bottle away.

"Why so little?" Denice moaned.

Nobody answered for a few moments. Then Atim blurted, "Grandpa gave us this package!"

"Where is he?"

Chickadee gave her older cousin another small sip and again, took the bottle away.

"He said he'd pray for you," Chickadee told her as she returned to rubbing Denice's back.

"But it's your quest, he said." Sam watched to see how his cousin would take that.

"My quest? I'm sitting on the company pier, getting slivers in my butt, and Grandpa thinks I'm on a quest?" Denice sounded annoyed. "Crazy old man. Sends me a sip or two of one of his potions. *Pfft!*"

The Muskrats were a little taken aback by their cousin's disrespectful words.

"Did he give me anything else?"

Atim reached back into the bag and pulled out a small packet of four salted crackers.

"Crackers?" Denice laughed. "My throat is so dry, I can't eat crackers."

"It's what Gramps gave us," Sam told her. "He said you picked your wilderness…for your vision quest. And now you have to see it through."

"Well…I'm sore. The thirst and the hunger aren't so bad. My shoulders are so sore. My legs. My back is on fire. Keep rubbing it." Denice winced as she changed the shoulder she was leaning against. Chickadee upped the pressure and frequency of her strokes along the older girl's back. It seemed weird to see Denice so weak.

Sam noticed a furious blotch of red rash where Denice's skin had pressed against the stained wood. It was then that he noticed his grandmother's blanket wasn't in sight.

Denice let out a sigh. "You guys are good kids." She lifted her head to smile at each of them. "That's why I'm doing this—so it's still here for you when you get to my age. They've made so many changes. And they never stop." She sat in silence.

Sam looked out over the pier. Men were working here and there, wherever a barge had docked along the thick wooden fingers that stretched into the lake. Behind him the warehouse overshadowed the scene like a great wall that blocked off this portion of the shore from the rest of the world.

The area smelled of diesel and wood rot. The action of moving the ore off the barges and loading it onto the trucks had caused many a minor spill. Now this ore-gravel was pressed into every nook and cranny of the wood and concrete pier. Denice was fastened to a dock pillar. A small group of boxes still sat in a half circle around the protest.

Samuel stood above Chickadee. She continued to

massage Denice's back. Atim looked down at the girls, his face drawn and worried.

"Where's Grandma's blanket?" Sam whispered. He was almost surprised that anyone heard.

Denice beckoned with her head. "Give me another sip." When she had finished what was left in the bottle, she went on. "I gave it to Steven. To put in his locker. I didn't want it to get dirty."

"Was that the guy from Smokey Bend?" Chickadee asked.

"Yeah, that's him." Denice laughed in spite of her aches. "Cute, hey? For a guy from Smokey Bend, anyway."

"He spoke to us at the Station. He said he talked to you." Chickadee smiled at her cousin.

"We talked," Denice replied. "He said he had good kids, too." She lost herself in thought for a moment. "That blanket is all we have of Grandma. She always told us our job in life was to provide a good life for our kids."

"That's what that guy from Smokey Bend said." Sam pictured his grandmother's face. Her only ambition was to be a help to the next generation and make sure they had everything they needed—heart, body, and soul. She had earned a name among their people that best translated to English as "everyone's mom."

"She always said to take care of your family." Denice shrugged as she looked up at Sam. "Steven is trying to take care of his family, but he needs this job to do it. I don't know…I wish he didn't have to do this…work for the company."

Sam shook his head. "The company provides him with a paycheck. Not too many jobs around here that pay as good." He had asked his cousins who worked for the company how much they made at the entry level. Few made it beyond that. It wouldn't get you rich, but you could provide your kids with a pretty good Christmas if you watched your pennies.

"I'm so tired." Denice sighed and leaned heavily on the pier. "I think I'm almost ready to give in. You know, look around, I didn't stop anything. Didn't even slow them down."

She lifted up her hands, imprisoned in the pipe. "My shoulders and hands ache more than my stomach. I think I'm ready…"

"WHAT ARE YOU KIDS DOING HERE?!" Mr. Makowski's voice bellowed from behind them. The Mighty Muskrats jumped.

CHAPTER 16

The Day Gets Warmer

"We're just..." Sam knew what he wanted to say but was too startled.

"They're just bringing me supplies so I can stay here for another four days!" Denice's defiant voice had lost its dry rasp.

"YOU KIDS GET OUT OF HERE!" The company manager was steadily walking toward them.

"I think we should go," Sam said to Denice. "We're leaving right now, Sir!" he called to Makowski.

Chickadee stood up. Sam could see was she angry that Mr. Makowski didn't care about their older cousin. Atim was also fired up. Sam stepped in front of both of them. "We haven't left her anything. We're just about to go. We just had to check on her.... Our grandpa said."

"You kids...again? Where is your uncle? He better be looking for my man, Pixton."

"LEAVE THEM ALONE!" Denice screamed.

"We don't know where Uncle Levi is," Atim shot back at the big man.

"This one is going to starve here." Makowski pointed at their cousin. "She's almost done." He laughed.

"You don't care!" Chickadee shouted at him.

Mr. Makowski pointed in the direction of the gate. "GET OUT OF HERE!"

Samuel kept eye contact with the man as he slowly turned. "Good-bye, Denice," he said as he left.

"Yeah, see you soon," Atim said with anger in his voice.

Chickadee bent down and gave her cousin a hug. She gave Denice's shoulders a quick squeeze as she stood and gave the manager a fiery look.

The Mighty Muskrats walked stiff-legged around the warehouse.

"That old man may be dead because nobody in this town cares." Makowski walked right behind them.

"We've been figuring out where he is since we heard about him," Sam shot over his shoulder.

"We care," Atim added. "We just don't think he is where they're looking!"

"Kids!" The company man snorted. "We've been all around those snake pits. We're going to push farther back into the bush today, if that's what you're talking about."

"You aren't even looking in the right place," Samuel said out loud.

The manager's frown deepened, but he didn't say anything.

The group arrived at the fence. Makowski motioned for his men to get out of the way as he swung the chain-link gate open. When the kids were through, he gave the gate a shove and turned to go back to the office.

The nice guard who'd let them in looked slightly chagrined as the gate clicked closed.

"I'll keep an eye on her," he whispered with a smile.

Chickadee looked back at the warehouse that blocked his view of Denice. "Please, take care of her," she said to both the universe and the guard. Turning away, she and Atim started walking down the road.

"Thanks." Sam nodded at the man and then he followed his brother and cousin.

★

In the rising heat of the spring day, Atim took off his jacket as he broke the silence. "Where are we going now?"

"Yeah," Chickadee said with a sigh. "I wish Otter was here."

Sam started pinching his chin. "I don't know where we're going."

Chickadee sighed again. Atim kicked at a rock. They kept walking down the dusty road.

"It's after lunch, and I didn't have much for breakfast." Atim rubbed his belly as he walked.

Sam and Chickadee ignored the hint.

"'Kay, maybe we need to look at this a whole different way." Sam felt under pressure to find a destination. "Who pulled out that rope? Maybe…it wasn't Dr. Pixton."

"Mr. Mackie rented out the boat." Chickadee nodded, interested in Sam's line of thought.

"I don't know…I'm wondering why we can't find Fish." Atim swung his head to move his hair so he could see his brother clearly.

"That old man has been gone for…three days, two nights now. We haven't found Fish for the last two." Sam pinched his chin.

"His wife said he was around," Chickadee said.

"She'd lie for him," Atim reasoned.

Nobody disagreed.

"Should we go bang on his door again?" Atim asked.

Sam was deep in thought. Mr. Mackie was an old Métis fisherman with an extra boat. He didn't seem like someone who would do away with an archeologist. Fish had always seemed harmless, but he did have cousins and a brother who had been in trouble with the law…on more than one occasion. "If we go to his door again, maybe we should get Mark."

"Yeah. Good idea." Chickadee nodded vigorously.

Atim shrugged and flicked his hair out of his eyes as

though he didn't care, but he didn't object to the suggestion of a bodyguard.

"If we go get Mark, we'll pass by Grandpa's and see if his guests have arrived," Sam offered. The other two nodded and smiled.

With a plan of attack, three Mighty Muskrats hurried into the dark forest that lined the trail to their grandfather's. As they ran, they thought of Otter and wondered if he had found anything.

★

When the trio emerged from the bush, they came out onto another dusty, white gravel road. Looking down the hill at the houses built along the sloping road, they could see their grandfather's property closest to the shore of Windy Lake. There were unfamiliar vehicles in Grandpa's driveway.

With big grins, the brothers and their cousin began to run a little faster.

"Grandpa's guests!" Chickadee squealed, as she tried to keep up with Sam. Atim didn't bother to wait and sped off down the hill in a cloud of fast-moving dust. By the time his brother and cousin caught up to him, he was catching his breath in the front yard.

They burst into their Grandpa's home as one, tripping over themselves as they pushed through the door. The sudden squeak of the old wood and the commotion of the children caused the Elders inside to smile. They sat at the table—two old men and two women—having tea with Grandpa.

"Here they are," their grandfather said, watching their entry with pride.

Otter stood near him.

"Otter!" the three exclaimed as they saw him.

"What did you find out?" Samuel pulled his jacket off eagerly.

"Are you okay?" Chickadee asked.

"Thanks for leaving me behind!" Atim scolded with a grin.

"We have guests!" Grandpa said with mock seriousness. "Introduce yourselves!"

"Sorry, Grandpa." Chickadee rolled her eyes as she gave Otter a welcome hug.

The Mighty Muskrats lined up near their grandfather.

"This one, the girl...is Chickadee." Grandpa pointed at her with his lips.

"Hello! I hope your trip was good!" Chickadee said to the Elders with a smile.

"She makes good bannock. And good tea too," Grandpa told them. "This one," he pointed at Sam, "is Samuel. He's a thinker, but sometimes...he thinks too much. Eh, Samuel?" Grandpa chuckled at Sam.

"Thankfully, I have you to correct me, Grandfather."

Sam laughed. He turned to the guests. "I hope you enjoy your stay."

"This big one is Atim. He can lift one of those middle-sized boat motors already. Runs like a deer." Grandpa smiled at the tallest Muskrat. Atim nodded and grinned at the Elders.

"And you've already met my boy, Otter." Grandpa's pride in Otter was evident. "They call them the Mighty Muskrats." He laughed. "Funny, hey?" Grandpa said it like there was a hidden joke that only the Elders would know. After a good chuckle, Grandpa touched Otter on the shoulder. "Tell the other Muskrats your news!"

With a huge smile, Otter announced, "I found out who took the rope out of the boat!"

CHAPTER 17

Thinking Like a Bird

Otter began studying the land as soon as he pulled up the canoe. Somewhere here, there was a clue, if only he could find it. The trampled grass and brush around the snake pits parking lot testified to the search by the RCMP and the company men. Otter hoped any visible clues hadn't been trampled by the workers' big, steel-toed boots. Otter figured it wouldn't be long before they were here again. He knew that his grandfather was genuinely concerned that they would find and damage the Refuge. Otter hadn't seen it, but if Grandpa thought it was important, then it was important.

The morning chill was gone, and the heat of the day was increasing. Winter had held on as long as it could, but it seemed spring was rushing in after the storm a few days ago.

Otter thought of the hawk and the birds and looked

skyward. In the distance, hovering over the trees with its steady gaze focused on the ground, a red hawk balanced on the wind. *If that hawk lived on snakes,* Otter thought, *he must have been hungry due to the long winter.* He hurried over the graveled trail to the snake pits.

Eventually, the skinny spruce trees gave way to an opening covered in grass and brush. A few car-sized pits in the limestone surrounded a bigger one about the size of the house. These were the snake pits. From the rustling in the grass, Otter knew a few of the snakes were already awake. A few more days of this heat, and the whole area would be slithering with newly aroused reptiles.

Carefully, Otter inched toward the edge of the biggest pit and peered over. The archeologist wasn't down there.

Suddenly, the hawk screeched. Otter felt the raptor was angry at his intrusion, but it continued to study the earth. A ridge of bare limestone was the highest point around and the hawk was hovering over this area.

Leaving the snake pits, Otter made his way over to the ridge. He watched the grass carefully, making sure not to step on the few sluggish snakes that were early risers.

Otter stepped onto the limestone and glanced over his shoulder at the lower landscape. His back was to the bush on the edge of the casually groomed area that de-fined the snake pits as a tourist attraction. Investigating the limestone shelf where he stood, he noticed a clump of something black sticking to the rock a short distance away. Going closer, Otter soon realized it was the corpse of a garter snake that had come out of the pits. The snake's skin didn't look punctured. Instead, it looked like the snake had burst, its insides forcing their way through. Some of the flesh had been picked over.

The hawk screamed again. Otter looked up. The raptor hovered tirelessly, committed to watching the earth below.

★

"And that's when I knew what the birds knew." Otter paused and smiled at his cousins.

"What did the birds know?" Atim scratched his head.

Chickadee smiled. "I know what the birds know!"

Sam glared at her then grinned. "What do the birds know?" he conceded.

"The birds know you can kill a snake if you lift it really high and drop it," Otter said triumphantly.

Sam shook his head. "What does that have to do with finding Dr. Pixton?"

Grandpa laughed. "This one can't think like a bird," he said to his friends.

"The snakes that come out of the pit are mostly black...." Otter paused waiting for his cousin to catch up.

The room was quiet as Samuel pinched his chin.

Suddenly, understanding brought joy to his face. "Just like the shore rope from the rental boat!" he said with a big clap of his hands.

"Yes!" Grandpa laughed. The other Elders also clapped their hands and chuckled with their friend.

"That's great, Otter!" Chickadee slapped her cousin on the back and then gave him a hug.

"Now we can prove who pulled the boat ashore!" Sam said to Atim.

"Wait. What? What did Otter figure out?" Atim's forehead furrowed with confusion.

"Tell him!" Sam exclaimed.

"Sheesh! Tell him!" Chickadee rolled her eyes.

Otter, not used to being the center of attention, spoke quietly. "Well, when I saw the burst snake, I thought it might have burst because it was dropped. And there was a hawk hovering there, hunting. And, I didn't see it, but I bet when he does catch a snake, he flies way up, and then lets it go. It falls. And the hawk doesn't have to fight it to eat it. It can just pick over the bones."

"Okay, so…" Atim still wasn't getting it.

Chickadee hit him on the shoulder. "The birds picked up the rope from the boat, Goofy."

Atim thought for a moment and then grinned as the pieces suddenly fell into place.

Sam summarized everyone's thoughts. "So the rain-on-snow event was enough to pick up the boat and get it floating, then the storm pushed it across the lake, and when the storm stopped, the water went down and left the boat on the delta. And then, some bird thought the rope was a snake and picked it up. But he could only get so far. Being a bird, he couldn't lift the boat. So, when he dropped the rope, it was stretched out, just like someone had been pulling the boat in to shore."

"A-ho!" Grandpa said with a big smile. "The Mighty Muskrats have solved one again!"

Chickadee touched Samuel's arm. "We have to tell Uncle Levi!"

Otter laughed. "I already did!"

"When?!" his cousins asked as one.

"When I was coming back in the canoe. Gus was riding out to the snake pits with the RCMP. He saw me and stopped. That's when I told him."

"Way to go, Otter!" Atim slapped him on the shoulder.

Otter continued. "Gus told the RCMP…. They didn't hear what I was saying even though they were right beside Uncle when I told him."

"So, they've changed locations?" Grandpa's brow furrowed.

"As far as I know. I told them about the high water lifting the boat and about the snake."

Grandpa grinned. "You did it, Little One!" He gave Otter's shoulder a squeeze.

Samuel was excited to get going. "Our look on the

Internet suggested that Dr. Pixton was probably blown from the northeast shore."

Grandpa looked at his older guests. "So, should we go get our lazy bones out to look for this old man in the bush?"

The Elders nodded vigorously.

"We can go tell Charlotte's family, and they'll go out to cultural camp." One of the lady Elders indicated the other couple with a point of her lips. They agreed with much nodding and furrowed brows. Their chairs scraped against the wood floor as they stood.

"Who's taking care of that land?" one of the Elders asked.

Grandpa thought for a moment. "Windy Lake is big. There's a lot of land up there. A few families steward that land. Ol' Relic has a trapping cabin back there. The dog sled race goes right past it."

The Elder laughed. "Well, if Relic catches him, there's a good chance we'll just get that doctor's skin back."

"Don't say that!" His wife playfully hit him with her purse.

Everyone laughed.

"So, are there trails out that way?" another Elder asked as she put on her coat.

"Well…yeah, there're trails and those lines the survey-ors cut back in the old days. The bone-digger shouldn't be hard to find if he started out on one of those." Grandpa looked around and took stock of what was in his pockets, so he didn't leave the house without something he needed.

"You kids go find Mark and tell him to get a boat ready." Grandpa opened the door and stepped out. His guests followed.

With the grown-ups gone, the rest of the Mighty Muskrats gathered around Otter.

"You did it, cuzzin!" Atim shook Otter's shoulder.

"You didn't actually see the hawk lift the snake up?" Sam was curious.

"No, just the burst one on the ground. It was pretty gross... but cool, you know?" Otter grinned from ear to ear.

"I knew you'd figure something out." Chickadee gave him an affectionate shove.

"Well...now we should go find Dr. Pixton!" Otter announced.

"Let's put this case to bed!" Sam punched the air.

CHAPTER 18

Searching Slump

It took a couple of hours of preparation before everyone was in the boat. But eventually, the Mighty Muskrats stepped onto the northwest shore of Windy Lake in their quest for the archeologist.

As usual, Otter was first out of the boat, but he was followed closely by the other Muskrats, their older cousin Mark, and their grandfather.

Once on shore, Grandfather smiled wearily. He went over the details of this land that he had taught to them long before. "This is near where our ancestors used to camp in the winter. The town's sitting on our summer camp. This was closer to the muskrat fields...before the dam was built."

"You think the bone-digger is here, Grandpa?" Atim's voice was strained as he helped Mark pull up the boat.

"I bet there's a better chance of finding a history thief

at the old winter camp than at the snake pits." Mark knelt in the lake to wash the dust off the rope.

"Shhh," Grandpa scolded the oldest cousin. "Right now, he's just a scared old man. You don't know how the bush can frighten a city person. It's easy to say you are not afraid of the dark when you can flick on a light. We need to find him."

"Hi! Uncle Levi!" Chickadee yelled excitedly. Their uncle waved casually, as he stood among a group of RCMP officers, volunteers from the community, and company men.

They stood at the back of the crowd and listened to the federal officer detail the new search strategy. When it was over, people broke into smaller groups. Half of them got back into their boats and headed toward the sun dance grounds farther along the shore. Of those left, most of the Elders marched off to the nearby winter camp, some volunteers and company men headed down the few visible trails, others formed lines and started combing the bush along the shore.

When the crowd cleared, Grandpa went to Uncle Levi, and the Mighty Muskrats followed.

"Those people are going to trample all the signs." He pointed at one of the groups combing the bush.

"We're doing this by the book, Pops," Uncle Levi said seriously. "It took Gus and me a while to convince them that the hawk idea was possible. They didn't even tell Makowski the reason they're changing the search site."

Grandpa didn't push his son. He had dealt with by-the-book people before.

"Where do you want us to go?" Sam asked. The other kids nodded enthusiastically.

"Well, why don't you follow me?" Uncle picked up an ax and some gear and slung it over his shoulder. "I saved a trail for us to go down. It goes past a few traplines and two or three hunting cabins. It's down this way." He pointed toward a surveyor's trail.

"That's not the way to Relic's?" Grandpa asked, although he already knew the answer.

"No. He's over there more. I didn't think you'd want to bump into that old grouch. Not with the Muskrats."

Grandpa nodded. "Sounds good," he said and started off with a walking stick in hand.

The Mighty Muskrats followed.

Back when the dam was first built, teams of surveyors had measured, mapped, and cut great swaths into the bush. Long straight lines sliced through the spruce for miles and miles. They became part of the main trail system that had lain on the land since traditional times. The Elders didn't like the newer cuts because they made it easier for the wolves to catch the moose. But now and then they came in handy. Uncle Levi was taking them to an old trappers' trail that ran off of one of these.

Once they were on the trail, it didn't take long before Grandpa delivered his judgment. "He's not down here."

"We're not just going on tracks, Pop. We're going by the book remember?" Uncle Levi yelled over his shoulder, not breaking his stride. "I'm supposed to talk to the people who hunt out here. See if anyone is staying in the cabins. See if they saw anyone out here."

"Uh-huh." Grandpa sounded skeptical.

The Mighty Muskrats smiled knowingly as they listened to their uncle and grandpa verbally sparring with each other.

★

It was starting to get dark by the time they returned to their starting place. The rest of the searchers were there, waiting for further instructions.

Uncle Levi went and spoke to the head RCMP officer. Grandpa went to talk with his guests, who had just returned from the old winter camp with the other Elders.

The Mighty Muskrats and Mark found a quiet place to sit down. Their legs were tired from the long walk.

When Uncle Levi returned, he sighed. "They're sending the volunteers back home. They don't want anyone else getting lost. The doctor will have to spend another night in the bush. Where's Gramps?"

The Mighty Muskrats lip-pointed at the group of Elders closer to the boats.

"Come on." Their uncle beckoned. "You guys are going home, too. You did a good day's work today."

"What's going to happen to that old man, Uncle?" Chickadee's voice was filled with concern.

"I don't know." Uncle Levi's tone dipped low. "He's been lucky. Since the storm, the nights have been warm. Tonight is going to be even warmer, and it's too early in the spring for a lot of mosquitoes and blackflies. If the doctor is dry and uninjured, there's no reason he couldn't make it for a few nights out here. Hopefully, he has what it takes to survive one more."

Before he walked off to speak to the older volunteers, Uncle Levi beckoned to Mark. "You might as well get the boat ready." Their older cousin followed Uncle Levi down to the shore.

Otter yawned. The other Muskrats slowly pulled themselves up off the ground with groans and mutterings. After a stretch, Otter stood up and followed them to the boat.

Grandpa watched them. Chickadee's shoulders were slumped. Samuel's footsteps were heavy. Atim was staring off into space as he walked. Otter dragged his feet.

"I wonder how your cousin Denice is doing?" Grandpa said sternly.

That thought hit the Mighty Muskrats' hearts instantly, and they tried to put a little bounce in their step as they hopped into the boat.

CHAPTER 19

Two Visions Found

The next day, as Atim and Samuel arrived at Grandpa's for their morning chores, they came upon Chickadee and Otter who were already outside cutting kindling.

"One of those Elder couples stayed overnight, so there's lots to do," Otter said as he sliced off another sliver of wood with the hatchet.

"Hurry and come help, lazybones!" Chickadee barked.

The brothers laughed.

"What do you think we came to do?" Atim shot back defiantly.

The popcorn crackle of a vehicle coming down the gravel road drew everyone's attention. Uncle Levi's police truck came barreling around the corner. It skidded to a stop in the driveway.

"Come into the house, kids. Good news!" The truck's momentum seemed to have been absorbed by their uncle.

Grandpa's door opened with a *cr-e-e-e-k*. The Elders inside looked up from their tea to see Uncle Levi and the Muskrats parade into the kitchen.

"They found him!" Uncle Levi announced as he took off his cowboy boots.

"Yay!" Chickadee and Atim yelled.

"Ah-ho!" the Elders cheered, raising their teacups.

"Where?" Sam asked.

"Ol' Relic marched him out of the bush at the end of a shotgun! Called him a trespasser. The archeologist had broken into his cabin!"

"He's lucky to be alive!" Grandpa guffawed.

"I just heard it over the radio." Uncle Levi poured himself a cup of tea and leaned against the counter.

"Is he okay?" Sam asked.

"They say he is really hungry and cold, but other than that he's fine. And, like a new man, they said. I wasn't sure what that meant. The boys just said he was somehow different." Uncle Levi shrugged.

"We must go see Denice," Grandpa suddenly announced.

"That's where I'm going now," Uncle Levi said. "They're bringing Doctor Pixton to the company dock."

"Well, I think it's time to go check on your cousin. What do you think?" Grandpa smiled mischievously at the Mighty Muskrats.

Uncle Levi put his cup down. "I'm leaving now. I can't

be seen to have anything to do with you. The company people won't like it."

"Don't worry, we can get into trouble all by ourselves," Atim boasted.

"Sure we can," Grandpa agreed.

"I have no doubt," Uncle Levi shot back over his shoulder as he left.

"There's a package for your cousin in the fridge," Grandpa told Chickadee.

"It'll be good to see her," Chickadee said.

"She'll been done with her vision quest today. Let's go see what she learned." Grandpa grabbed his walking stick and headed out through the squeaky door.

It didn't take long for the Mighty Muskrats and their grandfather to get to the company docks. They had no trouble getting in. A large crowd, made up of the morning's volunteers, the company men, and the police officers, had gathered. Everyone waited for the RCMP boat to slide around the point and into view.

Grandpa led the children right to Denice. Her perch was at the shore end of the dock the crowd was on. Everyone would have had to walk past her to go down to the far end of the pier.

"Oh!" Chickadee said with both anger and concern as she knelt beside her older cousin. The boys stood around and fidgeted as if they weren't sure how to help, even though they wanted to.

"Grandpa!" Denice tried to shout, but the word came out as a dry croak. She was in even worse shape than the day before. Her back looked permanently bent. Her hair hung in dreads with clumps of creosote and tar stuck in it. She made a sorry sight, sitting cross-legged, arms wrapped around the rough, wooden pillar, hands locked within the metal pipe.

Atim began to rip open the bag with the water bottle inside, but Grandpa waved him off for a moment.

"How are you, Granddaughter?" Grandpa held her chin up and looked into her eyes.

"I want to go home, Grandpa. I'm tired." Denice looked up for a second but then hung her head, exhausted.

"Then all you have to do is let go, my child." Grandpa smiled.

"I don't know…Grandpa. Did I accomplish anything?" Denice's lack of energy was dragging down her emotions.

"Did you learn anything, Granddaughter?"

"I met a man from Smokey Bend," Denice explained. After a long pause, she went on. "He's a dad. Has two lovely girls. He works here. He needs his job. He says he needs the money to give his girls a better life. He makes me wonder…if I'm doing the right thing."

"You are fighting for what you believe in. That is rarely a bad thing," Grandpa assured her.

"Well, this is happening everywhere. The land is being sucked up by the city. Even if I stop it here…there are so many cities."

Grandpa shook his head and thought. He remembered a story that would teach without forcing a direction.

"Hmmm…. I once saw a beaver build a dam across a fast-moving river." He held a finger in the air like it was a talking stick. "It was too fast for her to make a dam straight across. Any small amount of mud she put in place was swept away." He used his arm to wave the mud farther down an imaginary stream.

"So…she found a narrow spot where the river was bent." Grandpa curved his hand to mimic the river's change in flow. "There was an eddy there. And she made… big half circles of mud and sticks, like a *U*. She made that small eddy bigger. And slowly, adding little branch, after little branch, she was able to build a dam across that fast water. Maybe you need to find a narrow place where you can make your dam."

"Where?" Denice had tears in her eyes.

"A nation's law is supposed to be the will of its people. I think you need to go and speak to their lawmakers."

"The *government?*"

"If that's where the lawmakers are, then yes."

"I see what you mean, Grandpa. So…this was all worthless, wasn't it?" Denice's sadness was evident.

"Did you start out doing something you believe in?"

"Yes."

"Did you hurt anyone?"

Denice laughed. "Just me."

"Did you learn something?"

Denice thought. "Yes…yes, I did."

"Once you learned something, did you use that information to come up with a better way of doing what you want to do?"

"I think so."

"Then…this will only be worthless if you do not act on your vision." Grandpa stroked her hair.

Denice stared out across the lake, and then at the crowd of people waiting for the boat that held the rescued archeologist.

"How do we get you off of here? Where are the handcuff keys?" Samuel looked at the pipe as though it was a puzzle.

"Handcuff keys?" Denice smiled. "I'm just holding my hands together in here."

Atim laughed. "You mean they could have just pulled you off of there if they wanted?"

"I was going to use handcuffs, but I forgot them." Denice looked sheepish. She slid her red, raw hands out from the confines of the pipe. "Oh! The pins and needles!" The exhausted activist spread out her fingers and then made a fist.

"Wait till you try to stand up, cuz," Sam warned with a smile.

"Don't laugh at me!" Denice tried to raise her voice, but it was too hoarse. She managed to chuckle.

"Is it over? Is she done?" Steven from Smokey Bend suddenly stuck his head into the group.

"I'm just getting started," Denice stated. "But I'm taking the fight to them."

As Chickadee helped Denice straighten her legs, her older cousin moaned in pain.

Steven knelt down and rubbed her back.

The noise from the crowd farther down the dock suddenly rose. The RCMP boat had been spotted.

"Grandpa?" Sam questioned his Elder, eager to see and hear what was happening. The chatter grew as the sound of the approaching boat was heard.

"I'll sit with her," Steven offered. He looked at Denice with concern.

"Okay, Mighty Muskrats...go see them bring in the bone-digger." Denice knew the curiosity that infused her cousins. "I'll be okay."

The Mighty Muskrats paused until Grandpa nodded his permission. The boys took off down the dock to check out the crowd. Chickadee took her grandfather's hand and pulled him along.

The boys stopped outside of the circle. They were unable to see anything. But when Grandpa arrived, the crowd parted at the sight of him. The kids followed in his wake as he made his way to the front.

Uncle Levi and Gus were there. They smiled at the family as they came through the crowd. The Muskrats jostled for position in front of the forest of legs. The archeologist had finally stepped out of the RCMP boat and onto the dock.

Dr. Pixton was wrapped in a blanket. His skin was chalk-white and the veins on his hands stood out in blue. The doctor's spine was bowed from the weight of the experience. All of his energy was being spent shivering. He looked permanently cold.

"We have to get him to the ambulance!" the RCMP sergeant shouted. "He has hypothermia."

"Clear the way!" the company manager yelled.

Although the officer and Makowski were in a hurry, the doctor wasn't. He walked at a glacial pace, refusing to be hurried or put on a stretcher.

"I'll make it," he gritted his chattering teeth as spoke.

A TV news reporter from the Aboriginal Peoples Television Network appeared out of the crowd and shoved a microphone in Dr. Pixton's face.

"Doctor, what happened out there?"

"Leave him be! Can't you see he's weak?" Makowski's thick arm tried to sweep the reporter aside.

The young Native journalist stood her ground and

pointed the microphone at the manager. "Well, can *you* tell us what happened?"

Makowski suddenly realized that he was being taped. He straightened up and changed the tone of his voice.

"He told us he pulled ashore to go look at the Indians' …uh…the people of Windy Lake's old winter camp, but he got lost and never made it back to his boat."

Suddenly, the doctor stopped his determined march. The crowd hushed.

"I…am small." The old bone-digger took the reporter's arm and looked into her eyes. "But do you know how big it is? The universe…the wheels within wheels…the circle in the sky? I saw them!"

The reporter slowly took her arm back.

"You saw the *universe?*" She looked around at those in the crowd as though to confirm she had heard right.

"I was hungry. I was alone. Your people lived here… and survived!" The archeologist spoke as though it were a revelation.

The reporter looked uncomfortable and mumbled, "I'm Anishinaabe. My people are from down south…."

"What strength!" Dr. Pixton looked around at the crowd happily. Makowski opened his mouth to say something, stopped, started again, and then shook his head in bewilderment. He touched the doctor's back, urging him to walk on.

"What will you do now?" the reporter probed.

Dr. Pixton thought for a moment and laughed weakly. "No more field work for me. No more digging up the bones of Native people. It's time I met some of the living ones." He reached out, squeezed the reporter's arm sincerely, and then walked to the waiting ambulance. The doctor's change of heart was whispered through the crowd. Eager to hear more, everyone followed the old man as he was helped onto a stretcher.

As the ambulance was pulling out of the parking lot, the lead RCMP officer turned to the crowd and the APTN cameras. "I want to thank you all for volunteering to look for Dr. Pixton. We were able to bring him home due to your help!"

The people in the crowd cheered and patted each other on the back. The Mighty Muskrats looked at each other gleefully. Grandpa smiled and tousled Otter's hair.

The officer went on.

"We really want to thank the Windy Lake Police, Levi and Gus, for not only arranging the volunteers, but also giving us the information that helped us change our search location…and actually find the doctor. Come up here and say something, Gus."

Gus was a funny guy who was used to being the center of attention. "I'd like to claim the credit, I really would…." He shrugged. "But I have to give credit where credit is due. It was the Mighty Muskrats who figured it out."

A great "Oh-ho!" went up from the crowd. The RCMP

officer looked a bit chagrined. The Mighty Muskrats were pushed forward into the center of the circle.

Gus smiled at them and lined them up and patted them on the back. The APTN camera was rolling.

Gus spoke to the crowd and the reporter.

"We thought, from the way we found the boat, that someone had pulled it into the mud of the delta. But these kids figured out that wasn't the way it happened. How did it happen, Otter?"

Otter shielded his eyes from the camera's bright light. "Grandpa told us that if we wanted to know the secret, we'd have to know the delta and what the birds know. Well, the birds know that if you pick up a snake and drop it, you can kill it!"

The reporter had no idea what Otter was talking about. She waited expectantly. He smiled with a feeling of completion.

Chickadee pushed Sam forward.

"...And that's how we found out the boat's rope was pulled out by a hawk...and not Dr. Pixton, or someone who stole the boat. We also found out the rain-on-snow event followed by the dam opening was enough to lift the boat. Then the wind must have just naturally pushed it to the other side of the lake."

The reporter looked impressed. Denice and Steven pushed through the crowd. Steven had his arm around her waist and was helping her walk. They both smiled when they saw Denice's little cousins. Grandpa proudly watched his grandchildren from the edge of the crowd.

Sam continued. "That's when we figured a hawk saw the rope. It must have picked it up and tried to pull it high, but, of course, the boat was too heavy. So, the hawk dropped the rope, making it look like someone had pulled it out. Everyone was searching on the wrong side of the lake."

The RCMP officer, after hearing the whole story, smiled at the kids.

The reporter tightened up the line of Mighty Muskrats. Sam, Chickadee, Atim, and Otter hugged each other and giggled uncontrollably.

"There you have it, folks," the reporter said into the camera. "The case of Windy Lake has been solved by these kids, called..." She motioned to Sam as though he should say the name.

Instead, the four sleuths looked at each other and with a wide grin they yelled as one, "The Mighty Muskrats!"

ABOUT THE AUTHOR

MICHAEL HUTCHINSON is a citizen of the Misipawistik Cree Nation in the Treaty 5 territory, north of Winnipeg. As a teen, he pulled nets on Lake Winnipeg, fought forest fires in the Canadian Shield, and worked at the Whiteshell Nuclear Research Station's Underground Research Lab. As a young adult, he worked as a bartender, a caterer for rock concerts and movie shoots, and, eventually, as a print reporter for publications such as *The Calgary Straight* and *Aboriginal Times*. After being headhunted by the Indian Claims Commission, Michael moved from journalism to the communications side of the desk and worked for the ICC in Ottawa as a writer. He returned to his home province to start a family. Since then, he has worked as the Director of Communications for the Assembly of Manitoba Chiefs, and as a project manager for the Treaty Relations Commission of Manitoba, where he helped create the "We are all treaty people" campaign. Over seven years ago, he jumped at the chance to make mini-documentaries for the first season of *APTN Investigates*. Michael then became host of APTN National News and produced APTN's sit-down interview show, *Face to Face*, and APTN's version of *Politically Incorrect, The Laughing Drum*. Michael was recently in charge of communications for the Manitoba Keewatinowi Okimakanak, an advocacy organization for First Nations in northern Manitoba. He currently lives in Ottawa, Ontario where he continues to advocate for First Nation families and communities across Canada. His greatest accomplishments are his two lovely daughters.